FAMILY TENSIONS

THE FISCHER FAMILY TRILOGY BOOK 2

NAOMI TROYER

THE OUTSIDER

"Now that we have set a date for the wedding, let's make a toast to the happy couple." Edwina Fischer held up her glass of freshly pressed orange juice.

Edward Fischer reached for his glass and felt genuine happiness for his twin brother, Bram, who was marrying their neighbor's daughter, Lucy. They had suffered a troubling courtship at the start, due to Edward's confusion over his feelings for Lucy. But as he looked at the happy couple now, he knew that his feelings for Lucy had never even closely resembled the love she and Bram shared with each other.

It was early February, and the fire was cheerfully crackling in the hearth. It had been a colder winter than most, bringing more snow than their community had seen in recent memory. Outside you could hear the cold wind howling, as if upset because it had been shut out. But inside the Fischer home, it was blissfully warm as the entire family sat around the dining table.

Edward glanced at his younger sister, Daisy, who sat to his left, before glancing at his father who sat at the one head of the table, and his mother at the other. Across from him, Bram and Lucy looked more in love than ever before.

Edward held up his glass to the happy couple. "To Lucy and Bram, may your marriage be blessed, and your happiness endure the tribulations of life." Edward made the toast, meaning every single word.

There had been a time when he and Bram had been at odds with each other; for Edward, it had been the worst experience of his entire life. Once again, he and Bram were now the best of friends, supporting and understanding of each other's dreams.

Edward just wished there was a way that his father could do the same.

"May Gott bring you gut harvests, healthy kinner, and the patience it takes to make a marriage work," Samuel, Edward's father, said with a proud smile.

"Denke, we appreciate your gut blessings. But the wedding is a little more than two months away, first we have planting season to think of." Bram smiled at everyone around the table.

Edward could see the excitement in his brother's gaze. All his dreams were coming true. After Edward had admitted his true passion for cooking to his family, he had admitted to his father that he had never had the heart of a farmer.

The plan had always been to divide the farm between the two brothers, but instead, Edward insisted the land go to Bram. Bram was a natural-born farmer. He would do more with the land than Edward could ever dream of doing.

And Edward didn't dream about becoming a farmer at all.

Edward was still searching for his dreams, or rather, a way to make them come true. Whereas Bram was marrying the love of his life in less than a month, and come spring, he would be responsible for preparing, sowing, and harvesting the entire farm. It was a big responsibility, but it was one Edward knew Bram would succeed at.

Edward's future didn't lie in the land. He wasn't sure where exactly it would take him, but he knew that he wanted to cook. He wanted to spend his life creating new recipes, combining flavors that would both intrigue and satisfy any palate, and most of all, he didn't want to spend it working in a field.

His father was having a difficult time accepting that. According to Samuel Fischer, a frau belonged in the kitchen. Not a man.

Edward took a sip of his juice before he indulged in the lamb roast his mother had made for the occasion. He had offered to help, but regardless of his passion for cooking, his mother was still resistant to let him help with dinner.

It was bad enough that his father all but avoided him because of his love for cooking, but to have his mother almost shun him from her kitchen hurt even more.

"As soon as the ground begins to thaw, we can start plowing, Daed," Bram said, glancing outside. "I think it's going to be a late thaw this year. We might have to hire some help."

"Like I said, Bram, I have complete faith in your ability to bring in a gut harvest. You decide what you need to do to achieve that. If you need to hire on help, that is your decision too. Just keep in mind the cost of hiring farm workers and how that will affect your profit when the harvest comes in." Samuel spoke to Bram with respect and confidence in his voice.

"I will, Daed," Bram nodded in agreement. "But going on the expense of farm workers now will only increase our harvest."

"Like I said, I trust your judgement when it comes to the farm. A father couldn't be prouder than to have such a gut farmer as a seeh. There are some days where I think you're more apt at it than I ever was."

Bram and his father shared a look of respect and affection. It didn't seem to bother anyone else at the table, except for Edward.

When was the last time his father had looked at him like that? Would his father ever be proud of him again?

His father turned to him with a firm look. "Edward, since you're not interested in working the land, I expect you to pick up chores around the house. You can help your mother with the laundry, the dishes and the floors."

It felt as if his father had just slapped him right across the face. The one thing he wanted to do, cook, wasn't on the list of chores his father had just assigned to him. "Daed, I didn't say I'm not going to help. I just said I don't want to be responsible for bringing in a harvest or farming my own land. I'll work the land with you and Bram, as I've always done."

His father didn't comment, instead just huffed impatiently. "I thought you preferred a woman's chores?"

Edward bit on his tongue to stop himself from an anger outburst. He drew in a deep breath before he spoke. "I don't prefer a woman's chores; I simply hope to cook someday. Which means I wouldn't mind helping with meals."

"That's your mamm's decision. Enough about your lack of direction." His father turned to Bram. "Are you planning on sowing just corn this year, or do you have plans for other crops as well?"

"We have the seed for the corn, but I was considering maybe sowing a field or two with wheat or alfalfa. I haven't yet decided. I'll first need to work out the operation budget for the year if I'm going to hire help. I'll have to see if I can afford to purchase seed."

"Gut thinking," Samuel approved with a nod.

Edward felt as if he had become an outsider in his own family. He sat at their table, but it was as if he didn't exist to his father anymore. As the head of the household, his father had the power to either let you feel accepted and loved or ostracized and unwelcome.

Edward didn't have to doubt he fell into the latter category.

A DIFFERENT PERSPECTIVE

"*D*enke for dinner, Mamm. I'll begin clearing the table." Daisy, his younger sister by two years, began to gather all the dishes.

Needing to escape the glow of his father's disappointment and dismissal of him, Edward quickly rose to his feet. "Let me help."

Edward took the large stack of dishes from Daisy and carried them to the kitchen. He didn't even bother returning to the table to help her retrieve the rest of the serving dishes and empty glasses. Instead, he opened the faucet and began to fill the sink.

When Daisy returned with the second load, Edward was up to his arms in soapsuds.

"That's my job," Daisy said as she set down the stack of dirty serving dishes.

"I don't mind," Edward said under his breath. He needed an escape and right now, washing dishes was the best excuse he could find for not sitting at the table. Of course, his father would no doubt have something to say about that as well, because this too was probably a *woman's* chores.

Daisy shrugged. "If you don't mind, I won't argue. I'll start tidying up the kitchen and give you a few minutes to stew, but then we're talking about it."

Edward turned to her to argue, but she held up a finger. "We are talking about it."

Although she was younger than him, Edward had long since learned that if Daisy wanted to talk about something, short of fleeing to a different state, you wouldn't be able to stop her. Resigned, he continued to wash the dishes.

He couldn't help but feel lost, although he was home. He felt completely alone, although he was surrounded by family. Over the last few months, he had begged Gott to help him understand why he couldn't be like Bram.

Why he couldn't be son his father approved of? Why did Gott bless him with dreams he would never be able to follow? Why did Gott give him talent for something he could never practice? His faith had always been strong, but given his current situation, he couldn't help but wonder if Gott was punishing him somehow.

"Right, your five minutes are over. Everyone is in the living room by the fireplace, so now you're going to tell me, what's going on? You look like a dog whose bone has been taken away?" Daisy asked, coming to stand beside him.

"You know what's wrong," Edward muttered. "And there's no use talking about it, because you and I know that won't change anything."

"Daed," Daisy nodded. "Jah, it's hard to miss the way he dismisses you. I just didn't think he'd do it in front of company, especially Lucy."

"He's not even trying to hide his disappointment, Daisy. Perhaps it's better if I just leave..." Edward trailed off. The thought had occurred to him numerous times, but he pushed it aside every time. He didn't want to leave his community, or his familye. He didn't want to become Englisch and forsake his baptismal vows.

But he couldn't continue living his life in the shadow of Bram's success and in the scouring heat of his father's disapproval.

"And how would that change anything? Then you'll give him even more reason to be disappointed in you. I understand that he's making you feel as if you don't matter, but you do. Besides, don't be jealous of Bram. You didn't want to be a farmer," Daisy pointed out with a cocked brow.

"I know that Daisy. And I'm not jealous of Bram. I'm very happy for him and proud of him. I know that he'll be a gut farmer and bring in a gut harvest this year. I'm just... I don't know if Daed will ever accept that I don't want to be a farmer," Edward admitted as he rinsed the last dish.

"Edward, the only way he'll accept that you have other dreams is to prove to him that you're good at it. Cook a meal, get a job, do something that will show him that you're trying to follow your dreams," Daisy suggested with a hopeful look. "But instead, you've spent all winter feeling sorry for yourself and doing almost all the chores Mamm and I usually do."

Edward turned to Daisy with an agitated look. "How can I prove to him that I'll be a good cook if Mamm won't let me cook? If I find a job, it will probably be in a restaurant with an Englisch owner... can you imagine how disappointed Daed would be then?"

Daisy nodded in agreement. "I can see that you feel as if there is nowhere for you to turn, bruder, but remember, Gott tests us all in different ways. Stop thinking of your talent, your dreams, as a burden, instead turn to Gott to help you pass this test."

Edward smiled affectionately at his younger sister. "When did you get so wise?"

"I've always been wise. I just used to be too short for any of you to listen," Daisy teased. "And don't worry too much about Daed. He'll come around. Just give him time. Keep in mind that he spent his whole life preparing you and Bram for the farm. He must feel as if he wasted all that time and energy on you when you never even wanted to be a farmer. It will take time for him to accept that his dreams aren't yours."

"You're right," Edward nodded. Perhaps instead of blaming Gott for his talents, Edward realized it was time to ask Gott to lead him in a direction that he could pursue it. And instead of being angry at his father for his behavior, he should try to understand his father and be more patient.

"Gut, now let's cut the cake. Mamm baked my favorite chocolate cake, especially for tonight." Daisy clapped her hands with glee, reminding Edward of the little girl she'd once been.

"I'll fetch the plates."

Edward sliced into the cake and the rich scent of chocolate filled his senses. His mother's chocolate cake had always been the best in the community. But as Edward served the slices, his mind began to work.

How could he make it moister?

How could he enrich the flavor of cocoa?

What would he add to give the cake more depth, more complexity—perhaps berries?

"Come on, let's go eat cake!" Daisy announced when all the plates had a slice.

Edward followed her to the living room, hoping that one day he'd have the opportunity to try to bake his mother's recipe for chocolate cake, with a few adjustments of his own.

A ROSE-FLAVORED LIFE

*N*aomi Hostetler slipped the tray of freshly baked croissants out of the oven, and the rich scent of buttery goodness filled the kitchen. A smile curved her mouth, knowing that the croissants would taste even better than they smelled.

This was her second batch of blackberry and dark chocolate croissants. A combination her father doubted until Naomi proved him wrong by selling out the first batch within the first hour.

The Hostetler family had been bakers for three generations, and just like her ancestors, Naomi had been privileged to inherit the family passion and talent.

Ever since she could remember, she had been fascinated by the combination of ingredients, the scents, and the smiles on their customers' faces when they stepped into the store and saw the variety of baked goodness they offered.

The bakery had started as a small shop on Main Street almost sixty years before, but in time had expanded into so much more. The store itself was now three times the size of the original, with an industrial kitchen added onto the back.

On top of the bakery, her grandparents had been clever enough to have an apartment built, which was as spacious as the bakery. Because of the long hours and the difficult commute from the Amish settlement outside of town, living on top of their business had just made more sense.

Naomi was never more grateful for the intuit than on cold winter mornings, like today, when she began baking before dawn. There was no need to brave the snow and frosty wind. Instead she could just pad downstairs and indulge herself in the craft she loved.

She set down the croissants to cool before she slipped the muffin trays into the oven next. Muffins comprised most of their early morning sales, usually accompanied by a cup of freshly brewed coffee they served as well.

This morning they would feature various flavors, ranging from cappuccino to lemon spiced poppyseed. Of course, they would also offer the regular bran and banana muffins as well.

A glance at the clock on the wall revealed it was thirty minutes before the doors would open, which meant her father would be coming down at any moment. She had barely finished her thought when her father stepped into the kitchen. "Guten mayrie, dochder. Sleep well?"

Joseph Hostetler moved directly towards the coffeepot that was always brewing in the kitchen.

"Guten mayrie, Daed. Jah, very well. I dreamt of baking a cake, but not just any cake. A chocolate rose cake," Naomi said with excitement in her eyes.

"I know roses are edible, but do you think people will actually eat it?" Joseph said with a doubtful look.

"Not physical roses, Daed, layers of dark chocolate cake and between them, rose water flavored layers of cake. The rose water layers would be sweet in contrast to the bitter dark chocolate. And instead of butter icing, just a simple ganache," Naomi explained eagerly.

Her father chuckled and shook his head. "You remind me of your grossmammi when you speak like that. I've always enjoyed baking, but I prefer sticking to the recipes I know. Your grossmammi used to experiment and come up with the most interesting pastries."

"Really? At least I take after someone," Naomi teased lightheartedly.

For as long as Naomi could remember, it had just been her and her father. Her mother had passed away when she'd been very young, but her father had been so involved in her life that Naomi had never really felt as if she was missing something.

"And one day you'll take over the bakery after me," Joseph said with an affectionate smile.

"Luckily, that's a long time away. I love everything about the bakery, except for the office part. All those ledgers and numbers make my brain go fuzzy," Naomi admitted ruefully.

"For all the good the bakery gives us, we have to suffer the numbers as well," Joseph said wisely before he glanced at the clock. "It's time."

It had become a tradition for Naomi and her father to open the bakery together. While her father switched on the lights and powered up the cash registers, Naomi would stock the shelves and open the doors.

Together, they would welcome their first customer for the day. To some, it might seem foolish how fond Naomi and her father were of each other but it wasn't foolish to Naomi at all. She enjoyed working with her father and respected him as both a baker and a business owner. Although he played down his own talents, Naomi knew she would never be able to master a cheesecake the way her father did.

Or to raise a daughter alone.

She smiled at her father with love and admiration before she opened the doors at exactly eight o'clock.

LESSONS IN FARMING

A month later, the ground had begun to thaw.

After a very cold winter, there had been a surge of heat blowing in from the south, sending winter on her way and allowing spring to begin its magical transformation of the land.

Edward was still helping with the chores around the house, but now that it was time to start plowing the fields, he was at his brother's side. It was evident to Edward that Bram basked in the glow of his father's pride. Edward could clearly see a change in his brother as he took control of the farm.

He was decisive, eager, and planned on another record harvest for the Fischer farm. Edward admired his brother's courage, because taking over the entire farm was a great responsibility. In addition to the fields, the crops, and all the care needed to maintain them, it meant taking responsibility for his family's financial future.

One wrong decision could mean that his family and Bram's new wife would suffer the consequences. As a farmer of crops, especially corn, it meant your entire year's income depended on one harvest. An income that needed to last until the next harvest.

If the harvest didn't bring in enough profit, it would mean a difficult year for everyone.

But just like his father, Edward had complete faith in his brother's capabilities.

He enjoyed working with Bram. Unlike his father, who shouted orders and was always impatient with the way Edward worked, Bram treated him like an equal. When he wanted Edward to do something different, he would first explain why, before he showed him the right way.

It was easy to see that Bram would make a wonderful teacher for his sons one day. They would be privileged to have a father like Bram to teach them the ways of farming.

"I appreciate your help, bruder. I know we don't usually plow the fields twice, but we haven't rested these fields in a couple of years. Giving the dirt more oxygen and plowing in more surface matter will boost the fields for another couple of years before I need to rest them," Bram explained when they stopped working to rest the horse.

While the draft horse grazed nearby, Edward and Bram rested beneath a tree.

"Sounds like a clever plan. Daed never really rested any of the fields, did he?" Edward asked, curious about the differences between Bram's ideas and his father's.

"Nee. It's not necessary if you fertilize your fields every year, but fertilizing is expensive. I'd rather save on fertilizing this year and hiring on help," Bram explained.

"Ah, I see. Daed only fertilized certain fields every year," Edward nodded.

"Jah. That's why the southwest field yielded such a sallow crop last year. That field is overworked. I'm not planting corn there this year. I'm trying to find a crop I can plant there that will replenish the ground whilst bringing us an income."

Edward smiled at his brother with an impressed look. "Sounds like you really know what you're doing."

"I hope so, or you'll all go hungry next year," Bram chuckled, although Edward could see it was a real concern for Bram if he failed.

"You won't fail. You'll exceed all Daed's expectations," Edward promised him with a smile.

"And one day, so will you," Bram returned, meeting Edward's gaze. "What are your plans, Edward? You've distanced yourself from your half of the land, but you haven't done anything to pursue your dream of cooking?"

Edward shrugged with a heavy sigh. "I don't really know where to start. All the restaurants in town are owned by Englischers; Daed would surely disinherit me if I dare to work for one. Opening my own farm stall simply isn't an option without the money required to start. And the last option I considered would be dismissed by Daed before I even finish suggesting it."

"What's the last option?" Bram asked with a curious look.

"I considered cooking and baking from home. You know, birthday cakes, ready-made meals, stuff like that I could sell in the community. But Daed would rather have me shunned than sell baked-goods from home."

Bram nodded with understanding. "He's a difficult mann. Always has been. I agree, the last option probably isn't the best one. But you can't give up. If this is what you really want to do, Edward, then you need to keep searching for a way to do it. Even if that means working for an Englischer until you saved up enough to open a farm stall."

"Do you really think Daed will let me open a farm stall on the property?" Edward couldn't help but feel that all his ideas were filled with holes.

"Perhaps not right away, but if you explain it to him and the income you expect to make, he might be more favorable towards it," Bram tried to sound hopeful, but he was trying a little too hard.

Edward chuckled and shook his head. He appreciated his brother's support and advice but knew that Bram knew their father just as well as he did.

The fact that Edward wanted to cook, and bake was something their father was ashamed of. Edward didn't know how he could ever change his father's view.

"Can I ask you a really ridiculous question?" Bram turned to Edward with a questioning look. "Then we need to get back to plowing the field."

"I'm listening."

"You talk about your love for cooking as if you've done it for years, but have you ever really cooked, or baked for that matter? I've never seen you cooking in our haus, which leads to me wonder how you know you're gut at something if you haven't done it?" Bram tilted his head, curiously waiting for Edward's answer.

Edward smiled. "Lucy. I've helped her cook meals and I've baked my own recipes in their kitchen from time to time. That's how she knew."

Bram chuckled. "She's a better woman than I realized."

"She's special, Bram. You're very blessed to have her heart."

"I am, truly," Bram agreed, before his eyes widened with excitement. "I have an idea. Why don't you cook for Daed? Make dinner one night and cook everything you know he will love. But it has to be gut, even better than Mamm's cooking. That way you can prove your talent to him. Perhaps he'll be more willing to accept it then?"

Edward thought for a moment before he shook his head. "I don't think Mamm will let me. You know she always supports Daed. Letting me cook might make her feel like she's betraying Daed."

"You can ask," Bram insisted. "Otherwise, you can ask Lucy to use their kitchen."

"I might consider that. Denke."

"And don't stop searching for work, Edward. The sooner you're cooking full time, the better you'll become." Bram's words were encouraging.

Edward smiled at his brother. "And the sooner we continue plowing, the sooner you can sow."

A SPITEFUL COATRACK

"*D*enke for dinner, Naomi," Joseph said with an affectionate smile for his daughter.

Naomi chuckled and shook her head as she gathered their plates. "It was corn salad; it was hardly dinner."

"My mamm always said that any meal you didn't have to prepare yourself was a meal to be grateful for."

Naomi smiled at her father with promise. "Tomorrow night, I'll cook your dinner. But right now, I need to deal with these dishes before I go and finish that wedding cake."

"But it's done." Joseph argued with a frown. "What else do you need to do?"

"I'm not happy with the bow or where it attaches to the ribbon. It's going to bother me until I fix it."

The wedding cake was a much less elaborate one than the usual ones they baked on order. The bride and groom wanted a four-tiered lemon-blossom cake with a simple ribbon tied around the tiers. On top of the cake, there would be real lemon blossoms the bride would provide, along with a pair of rings made from fondant. Naomi had suggested adding a bow, to which they had eagerly agreed.

Now she could kick herself for the suggestion because she couldn't get it exactly right.

"You go on and fiddle with that ribbon. I'll do the dishes. Don't stay down in the bakery too late," her father urged before he stood up. "I'm going to read for a while before I turn in."

"Jah, I won't. Sleep well, Daed." Naomi started towards the door that led to the staircase. "Denke for the dishes."

When Naomi reached the bottom of the staircase, she flicked on the lights to the kitchen. She had spent many nights working in that kitchen and had never complained about it. She enjoyed the silence, the absolute stillness hanging over the town, while she allowed her creativity to flow.

Often during the day it was too busy for her to be able to focus when she was working with fondant.

To Naomi, it hadn't felt like ten minutes had passed, but when she glanced at the clock, she realized she'd been working for the last hour. She had created a new ribbon, and the bow looked perfect this time.

With great care, she removed the old ribbon from the cake and gently draped the new ribbon around it. Its width was better and the color a brighter shade of yellow than the other one had been. It stood out against the white fondant.

She touched the bow and made sure it was dry enough to handle before she carefully, holding her breath, situated it against the ribbon. She held it in place until the piping gel took hold. The curved parts of the bow were still soft enough for her to shape it again before inserting small pieces of foam to allow it to dry.

Naomi stood back and her mouth curved into a satisfied smile.

Now it looked exactly how she had wanted it to look in the first place.

There was a thud upstairs and Naomi rolled her eyes, knowing her father had probably knocked over the coatrack again. He did it almost every night. For some reason, he couldn't walk past the coatrack without kicking its feet and sending it to the ground.

But when the thud was followed by a muffled cry for help, Naomi knew something was very wrong. The wedding cake long forgotten, Naomi rushed up the stairs, wishing they used electricity there as well.

After having her eyes adjusted to the bright lights of the kitchen, it took a moment for her eyes to adjust to the faint lantern light. Although they had permission from the bishop and the elders to use electricity in their business, they still refrained from using it in the apartment unless absolutely necessary. They didn't have a woodstove like most Amish folks, and instead made use of a gas stove and oven.

"Daed?" Naomi asked as her eyes began to scan through the apartment. The first thing she noticed was that the coat rack was still on its feet. She checked the dining room before she moved to the kitchen. When she still couldn't find him, she called out again. "Daed!"

"Naomi, here, my bedroom," Joseph's voice was filled with pain.

Naomi ran down the hallway and opened her father's bedroom door without hesitation. Her breath caught the moment she saw her father lying on the floor. It was clear he was in a lot of pain.

"Daed, what happened?" Naomi asked, rushing to his side. She kneeled beside him, noticing he was pale.

"I'm not sure. One moment I was on my way to bed and the next moment I woke up on the floor. My leg, Naomi, it hurts." Joseph pointed towards his left leg.

Fear coursed through Naomi as she assessed the situation. "Don't move, Daed. I'm calling an ambulance."

"Naomi, just help me onto the bed," Joseph argued.

"Nee, you're not going to bed until you've seen a doctor. You could've fainted for any number of reasons and besides, they need to look at your leg."

Naomi ran through the apartment towards the stairs. She took them two at a time, reaching the office in record time. She picked up the phone and dialed 911, hoping they would come quick. Although her father was conscious now, she couldn't help but fear that something was terribly wrong.

After giving her address and a short explanation of what had happened and her father's condition, she hung up and rushed back to her father's side. It wasn't long before she could hear the sirens of an ambulance.

As soon as she showed the paramedics to her father, they began to work. There were monitors and gauges, and masks, so many things Naomi didn't understand.

"Is he all right? Please, someone, talk to me?" Naomi all but begged.

One of the first responders turned to Naomi with a kind look. "He's all right for now, but we'll know more once we get him to the hospital. Would you like to ride along with us, or is there someone you'd like to call?"

Naomi thought for a moment and knew that there was one person her father would want her to call. "I just need to make a phone call. Jah, I'm going to ride with you."

A few minutes later, Naomi was on the phone again. She dialed the number for the phone shanty closest to the bishop's house. It took five rings before someone answered.

There wasn't time for formalities or explanations, Naomi just blurted out the information. "Please tell the bishop that Joseph Hostetler has had an accident. He's all right for now, but they're taking him to the hospital. Denke."

She turned around and saw her father being carried down the stairway on a stretcher. Her heart jumped into her throat, fearing she would lose him.

"Daed, just hang on. We'll be at the hospital soon," Naomi said, following the stretcher.

Her father smiled at her weakly. "They think it might be my hip…"

"You'll be fine," Naomi promised. "They're going to take real gut care of you."

While they loaded her father into the ambulance, Naomi grabbed her purse and locked up the bakery.

Right now, nothing mattered but her father.

The bakery, the wedding cake, everything else could wait.

PROBLEM SOLVED

*B*ram and their father had left for town an hour before to visit the seed store. Edward's mother was at her weekly prayer meeting, and Daisy was babysitting today for a young mother.

Alone at home, Edward glanced towards the fields before he decided to surprise his mother and start clearing out her window boxes. Just like it would be planting season for the farm, his mother's impatiens, peonies, and marigolds could be sown in the next week.

The dirt in every window box was tilled, fertilized, and watered. Edward was just about finished with the last window box when his mother returned from her prayer group. His mother didn't like driving the buggy, and only did so when she went to the prayer group. It was only two miles away and not once did his mother have to turn onto the Englisch roads.

"Edward! You readied the window boxes for me. How thoughtful of you," Edwina smiled when she reached Edward.

"Jah, you can start sowing your seeds in the next week," Edward pointed out.

"Denke. Now do your mamm another favor and drive her

into town. You know how I feel about driving in traffic." Edwina rolled her eyes. "Englisch drivers believe the road only belongs to them."

"What do you need in town?" Edward asked curiously.

"The bishop received a message last night that Joseph Hostetler, the baker, was rushed to the hospital last night. The bishop would've gone himself, but he's down with a terrible cold. I offered to go and pay Joseph a visit on the bishop's behalf," Edwina explained.

Caring for the community and offering support when needed was integral to their community. Edward knew that by supporting their community, if they ever needed it, support would be offered in return. "Of course, Mamm. Let me just wash up and we can go."

Almost an hour later, Edward and Edwina were shown to Joseph's room on the second floor of the hospital. Edward knew who Joseph was, and that he had a daughter, but he'd never been formally introduced. Their community was a large one and although you knew *of* everyone, you couldn't *know* everyone.

His mother pushed opened the door and whispered. "Can we come in?"

A young woman's voice answered. "Mrs. Fischer, please do."

Edward followed his mother into the room. Mr. Hostetler lay on the bed with a stubborn expression. His daughter, Naomi, sat at his bedside, looking very concerned.

"I'm so sorry; we heard of your troubles. The bishop would've come but he's down with a cold. What happened?" Edwina asked, moving to Joseph's other side.

"Nothing to be worried about. I'll be just fine. No need to concern yourself," Joseph insisted with a smile.

Edward wasn't sure Joseph was telling the truth, judging by the look on his daughter's face.

Naomi didn't speak to him or his mother, instead, she turned to her father. "Daed, stop saying that. It's serious." She turned to

Edward and his mother and let out a heavy sigh. Edward saw the shadows beneath her eyes; if he had to guess, he would say she hadn't slept all night. "The doctors say he suffered a mini stroke. A transient ischemic attack. It could be a precursor to a bigger stroke. They're treating him now to prevent that, but the real problem is his hip. When he lost consciousness, he fell. The radiology report just came in. He broke his left hip."

"Oh, my gutness, Joseph. Naomi is right, it is rather serious. Are you in a lot of pain?" Edwina asked, duly concerned.

"Nee, I'm not in pain. I told the doctors I'm fine to go home, but they won't listen," Joseph huffed in frustration.

"You can't go home," Naomi argued. "I'll be worried sick; it's better you stay here until everything is sorted. They're operating on him tomorrow. He'll need pins or something like that in his hip," Naomi explained.

"She's right Joseph, you need to take care of yourself. I know how frustrating it is to be in a hospital, but it's for the best. I'm sure Naomi can manage the bakery very well on her own," Edwina tried her best to encourage him.

"Sure, she can manage the bakery jah, but she'll need help. She can't lift the bags of flour, she can't bake and serve customers at the same time, and I don't feel right knowing she's there all alone all day. It's too much work for one person." Joseph sighed and shook her head. "So you see, I need to get out of the hospital."

Edward could understand Joseph's concern. The bakery was always busy and with only one person, it would be a lot of work. His mother glanced at him with a curious look.

"Joseph, I have a wunderbaar idea. Bram and Samuel will manage on the farm just fine without Edward. Edward can help Naomi until you're back on your feet again. Won't you Edward?" His mother's gaze made it clear he didn't have a choice.

"Uh, jah. I don't mind helping Naomi if it will give you peace of mind," Edward said to Joseph.

Relief washed over Joseph's face. "You wouldn't mind? We'll pay you for your time, of course."

"That won't be necessary," Edward quickly held up his hand. "I'm just glad I can help."

"Denke Gott," Joseph smiled with ease. "Edwina, you're a saint for coming to see me and for offering your seeh's help."

"It's only a pleasure. We'll let you rest." Edwina turned to Naomi. "What time should Edward meet you at the bakery in the morning?"

"I uh… eight o'clock should be fine," Naomi stammered, slightly caught off guard. "I can really manage on my own."

"And who'll run the bakery when you want to come and see your daed?" Edwina pointed out. "It's been arranged. Joseph, you take care and get well soon. Let us know if you need anything. Naomi, Edward will see you in the morning."

Edward bid farewell to the Hostetlers before he followed his mother out of the room. As soon as they were out of earshot, he turned to her with a baffled expression. "Mamm, this is a terrible idea. You know Daed won't approve."

"You and your father have been at odds for months now. Perhaps a little distance between the two of you is exactly what you need. Besides, I know it's not cooking, but you'll still be working in a kitchen."

Edward couldn't argue with his mother's reasoning. "All right, but you have to tell Daed it was your idea."

"Just leave your daed to me," Edwina smiled at her son with a wink of promise.

BULL IN A CHINA SHOP

As soon as the Fischers were good and gone, Naomi turned to her father with a horrified expression. "How could you agree with that?"

"What?" Joseph shrugged. "It's a gut idea, Naomi. You know there is too much work for you to handle on your own. Besides, Edward seems like a nice mann."

"Jah, there is too much work. Jah, he seems nice. But Daed, if I'm getting help in the bakery, I need someone that knows their way around a kitchen. Someone that understands the difference between a croissant and a coney roll. Not a farmhand better suited to steering a draft horse and plow than splitting eggs." Naomi paced up and down the side of her father's bed.

She was exhausted, both mentally and physically. She hadn't slept at all the night before. Ever since the ambulance had arrived at the hospital, she had been at her father's side. She had listened to doctors all morning and watched nurses come to check on her father every half hour.

Although her father pretended he was just fine, Naomi knew he was in a lot of pain.

The hip operation didn't sound very dangerous, but Naomi couldn't help but be concerned about that as well.

Right now, all she wanted was a good cry, a long bath, and a cup of warm tea. She didn't want her father accepting help from a farmer who would be like a bull in a china shop in her workspace.

"Naomi, I'm not going to argue about this. You're the one that insists I stay in the hospital and get the operation to secure my hip. Unless you want me hopping around the bakery with crutches, I suggest you accept that Edward is your only alternative," Joseph said firmly.

"But Daed," Naomi began, shaking her head.

"Nee. That's enough. If you don't want him in the kitchen, let him serve the customers. Our customers are regulars and will understand he's new. They'll be patient if he makes mistakes, I'm sure of it," Joseph explained. "All you need to do is bake your little heart out while he punches the cash register."

"But I have to teach him how to use it," Naomi complained.

"Then teach him. I know this situation isn't ideal, Naomi, but I need you to accept his help."

"All right, I'll teach him," Naomi finally sighed with resolve.

"And you pay him wages, daily wages, you hear? It's not like we can't afford to hire on help and he's turning his back on their farm to help us, so we make it worth his while," Joseph insisted.

Naomi nodded. "I will."

"Gut, now go home. As soon as that wedding cake has been collected, I want you to close the bakery and go upstairs. You need to rest; you've had a long night. You can start fresh in the morning," Joseph said with a kind smile. "Denke for everything. I appreciate you staying the entire night."

"Of course, Daed, where else would I have been?" Naomi reached for his hand and squeezed it tightly. "I'm too tired to even argue about closing the bakery for the day."

"Gut. Have the nurses call a driver for you."

Naomi nodded before she hugged her father goodbye. "Good-luck with the operation in the morning."

"Denke." Joseph smiled warmly at Naomi before she left his room.

Out in the corridor, Naomi took a moment to steady her racing her heart. Tears were near, threatening to spill over at any moment, but she would hold them back until she was home. She wouldn't admit to her father how afraid she had been when she'd seen him lying on the floor.

She was just grateful he was now in the care of capable doctors and nurses.

Naomi drew in a deep breath and vowed to make the best of a terrible situation. She knew that a farmhand would hardly be of any help in a bakery, but to appease her father, she would try to teach him to run the cash register. At least with someone helping customers, she could tend to all the baking.

She didn't really know Edward Fischer all that well, except that he had a twin brother and that their farm was the biggest in the community.

A yawn escaped her, and Naomi pushed all thoughts of Edward aside. She would worry about him tomorrow. Right now, she just wanted to get home and go to bed.

MINDFUL MANIPULATIONS

*E*dward sat at the dinner table; his palms clammy with sweat.

His mother had told him not to say a word about the bakery or helping Naomi, and instead to leave it to her to make his father understand it was for the best.

They had been home all afternoon and his mother had yet to say a word. The last thing Edward wanted was another argument at the dinner table about what a disappointment he was as a son. He pushed the food around his plate and ignored Daisy's curious looks while everyone else ate.

Suddenly, his mother set down her fork and gasped. "Ach, Samuel! I completely forgot to tell you I was at the hospital today."

Edward couldn't help but smile at his father's reaction. Samuel dropped his fork and met his wife's gaze with concern. "Are you all right? Did something happen?"

"Nee, nee. I'm perfectly fine. But something did happen," Edwina said in a mysterious way. "You know our dear baker, Joseph?"

"Jah, we were in school together. I remember him well," Samuel nodded.

"He had a terrible accident last night. The prayer group asked me to go and see him to offer the bishop's support."

Edward wasn't sure what his mother was doing, but she was taking her time getting to the most important part of the conversation.

"Is he all right?" Samuel asked with concerned curiosity.

"He is for now, but he'll be in the hospital for quite a while longer. They said he had what they call a mini stroke, it could be a precursor to a bigger one. So, you can understand why he needs to stay there. And his hip, I haven't even told you about his hip. When he had the attack, he lost consciousness and fell. The angle he fell at caused him to break his hip. They're operating on him in the morning. His poor dochder is simply falling apart with concern for him."

"I can imagine. It seems like he is going to take a long time to recover after all of that."

"Not just that," Edwina emphasized with wide eyes. "Think about the bakery, Samuel. It's their livelihood, their income. Naomi is a dear girl, but she could never manage it all on her own. And the last thing poor Joseph needs now is financial concerns, while he needs to focus on getting better."

"Sometimes fate really does curve the road with impossibly tight turns. I can only imagine how horrified Joseph must be to be stuck in hospital while his business suffers," Samuel sympathized.

"I know, he's afraid that if Naomi doesn't manage, they'll lose too many loyal customers and have to close the bakery." Edwina's voice held a warning tone.

Edward frowned, not sure the situation was desperate, but he didn't say a word.

"It would be a great loss for both our town and the community if the bakery had to close. It's been there for three generations. It would be like our familye losing the farm." Samuel's eyes widened with sympathy for Joseph.

"I know. That was why I couldn't help but agree when Joseph asked if Edward could help Naomi in the bakery until he was back on his feet. I wanted to suggest he ask Daisy instead, but the bags of flour are too heavy for a woman to carry. And Joseph insists he'll feel more at ease knowing there was a man in the bakery if any trouble should arise. I know our town doesn't really have any crime, but you never know when a robber or two might pass through, and then poor Naomi would have to face them alone," Edwina exaggerated further.

"I see. And have you spoken to Edward about this?" Samuel asked, turning to his son.

Edward felt his father's gaze on him and wasn't sure how to react.

"Nee, I thought it best to discuss it with you first. But of course, I knew that you wouldn't object. We've always done our part to help the community and the Hostetlers need our help now. Besides, you said yourself the other night that you and Bram have decided to hire on help for the sowing season, so you won't need Edward on the farm."

Edward watched his father's mouth open to protest before he closed it again.

"You wouldn't mind helping, would you, Edward? I know it would be tedious for you spending all day cooped up inside and lifting heavy bags of flour, but it would really help the Hostetlers?" his mother turned to him with a questioning look as if she were asking him for the first time.

"I, uh, nee, I don't mind. That is, if Daed agrees that they don't need me on the farm. The farm comes first, especially this time of year," Edward said, turning to his father.

Edward now realized the gentle manipulation his mother had planned. She turned to Samuel with a pleading look. "They could lose the bakery, Samuel."

31

His father shrugged and finally nodded. "I can't say I'm thrilled not to have Edward in the fields this time of year, but you're right. We need to help where we can. Perhaps Edward is more useful at lifting bags of flour than he is running the draft horse with the plow," Samuel ended with a scathing tone.

Edward refused to react to another one of his father's hurtful comments.

"Wunderbaar. Edward, you should be at the bakery at eight o'clock. Naomi will be so grateful for your help." Edwina smiled at her son with a triumphant look. "Besides, it will probably only be for a couple of weeks. I can't imagine they'll keep Joseph in the hospital much longer than that."

"Then it's settled," Samuel said, excusing himself from the table.

Edward turned to his mother with a look of admiration. "You have to teach me how to do that."

Edwina chuckled with a loving look for her son. "That's not something you teach, it's something you learn from experience. And I have had a lot of experience when it comes to having your father seeing things my way."

Later that night, Edward lay in his bed in the loft. Bram was already fast asleep on his side of the loft, but Edward's mind was racing. He couldn't help but feel excited about working in a kitchen. Then, of course, there was Naomi...

Edward didn't know her very well, but he found himself intrigued by her. She had a quiet type of beauty, the kind that became more pronounced the longer you looked at her.

He wasn't sure why, but he had a feeling that a door had just opened to his future. He wasn't sure where it would lead or what that future was, but hope swelled in his chest for the first time in years.

DIRT VS. DOUGH

$\mathcal{E}$dward said goodbye to the client and found himself glancing at Naomi.

It had been a busy morning, but now for the first time the bakery was completely empty. Except for the bride that was meeting with Naomi, there were no other customers to serve.

For a moment he stood and listened to the bride describe the cake she had in mind and the suggestions Naomi added to the bride's idea. Naomi was clearly very comfortable and confident in what she could do. A quality that Edward hoped he would one day have as well when it came to his own skills.

Knowing that Naomi had a lot of baking to do, and the bride was taking up more than double the time Naomi had planned to spend with her, he headed to the kitchen to see if he could help.

First thing this morning, Naomi had taught him how the cash register worked, before she had given him a tour of the bakery and the kitchen. She had a list of things she needed to bake today written on a whiteboard, and below the white board lay the recipe book that held all the recipes of the bakery. Generations of Hostetlers had written their recipes in the sacred book, one that was passed down from one owner to the next.

After checking the oven and the cooling racks, Edward consulted Naomi's list and saw that bran and banana muffins were next on her list of things to bake.

He didn't want to overstep, but he also knew that Naomi was running behind schedule. They hadn't really talked much that morning, but from what little time he had spent with Naomi, he had quickly learned that she didn't like falling behind on her baking. She baked on a strict schedule, to make sure the bakery was stocked with fresh items each day.

He considered for a moment, before he reached for an apron and opened the recipe book. He easily found the recipe he needed and began gathering the ingredients. There were bells on the entrance of the bakery, so should a customer arrive, he'd know to step out of the kitchen to assist them.

As he began to mix the ingredients, Edward found himself feeling relaxed for the first time in months. With ease he split the eggs, knowing that the recipe required the egg whites to be beaten separately to give the muffins an airy texture.

When all the ingredients had been prepared, he began to whisk through the entire batch. The scent of cinnamon, bran, butter, sugar, and bananas filled his senses. He could already imagine what they would smell like once baked. He spooned the batter into the muffin pans that had already been set out, before sliding them into the oven. Edward set the timer for twenty minutes before he returned to Naomi's list of things to do.

Next on the list was cocoa dusted chocolate truffles.

He retrieved the recipe and read it carefully, having never made anything of the sort before. He was intrigued that the recipe didn't require any baking, but instead refrigeration for four hours. Edward moved into the pantry and felt the rush of joy wash over him again. He had already been in the pantry numerous times that morning, but every time he stepped inside, his mind began to whirl with flavor combinations and ideas.

It was a feeling his father and his brother would never understand. But standing in the fully stocked pantry, Edward felt like a farmer looking at a month-old crop of corn, knowing the promise it held.

With his ears listening for the jingle of the entrance bells, he began to work.

"What are you doing?" Naomi asked, horrified as she stepped into the kitchen.

Edward looked up from kneading the dough for the truffles and smiled at her. "I'm making cocoa dusted chocolate truffles. I knew you were running behind, so I thought I'd help."

Naomi's eyes widened with fear. "Please tell me you know how to measure ingredients?"

"I do, and I did. Besides, the recipes are so meticulous, they're easy to follow." Edward shrugged. "Once I've finished kneading the dough for another two minutes, I can start forming the balls. They need to be refrigerated for four hours before they are dusted with cocoa and ready for the display in the front of the store."

Naomi's brows furrowed curiously. "You can bake?"

"I prefer to cook, but jah, I guess I can bake." Edward shrugged. The timer on the oven sounded and Naomi's gaze flew towards it.

"That's the bran and banana muffins. They're ready to come out," Edward said, wiping his hands before reaching for the oven mitts. "Don't worry, I did beat the egg whites separate until they formed peaks."

He retrieved the trays of muffins and set them on the cooling racks before turning to Naomi. "Do they get your approval?"

Naomi moved towards the cooling racks with a skeptic look. She looked at the muffins from all sides before she turned to Edward with a confused expression. "I couldn't have done it better myself."

"Denke," Edward said, feeling chuffed with her compliment.

The bells jingled on the entrance door, and Naomi and Edward glanced at each other. Before Edward set down the oven mitts, Naomi shook her head. "You finish those; I'll help the customer."

She hadn't said it outright, but clearly Naomi trusted him enough to let him finish another product. Her confidence in him made Edward feel like he was on top of the world. From what he'd seen that morning, she was a perfectionist when it came to both the kitchen and everything that left it. It felt good to know that she was pleased with what he had done.

Perhaps in time, she wouldn't be as unhappy about him being there.

It had been clear this morning that she hadn't been exactly thrilled to have him in the bakery. She had said outright that she couldn't see him being of much help and only accepted his presence there because it meant her father wouldn't worry.

Edward hadn't meant to prove her wrong, but it was clear he just did.

When she returned to the kitchen a few moments later, she looked at him with baffled curiosity. "I've never met a man who can cook, much less bake. Amish men simply don't care about that at all."

"I guess I'm different," Edward admitted wryly.

"Well, you've been a great help. I'll start on the next item."

They worked side by side in the kitchen for the rest of the afternoon, only leaving the kitchen to assist customers in the front. By the time the day came to an end, Edward helped Naomi clean the kitchen before he took a broom and swept the front of the store.

They hadn't spoken much, but instead of the stifling irritation towards him that Naomi had that morning, she now seemed almost glad to have him there.

Once he had done everything he could think of, he found her in the kitchen making tomorrow's baking list.

"Is there anything else I can help you with before I go?" Edward asked.

Naomi shook her head before her eyes widened. "Could you bring in a bag of flour from the storeroom? They really are too heavy for me to carry."

Edward chuckled. The flour had been the excuse everyone had used for him to be there, and now it was clear he was of much more use than just hauling bags of flour. "Of course."

Once he had deposited the bag of flour in the pantry, Naomi waited for him with an envelope in her hand. "Here are your wages for today. I really appreciate all your help."

Edward shook his head. "I don't expect you to pay me. I won't accept it. I enjoyed helping and don't mind helping until your daed is better."

Naomi tilted her head with a curious look and a ghost of a smile. "You're nothing like I expected Edward. You keep surprising me. Either way, you weren't just in my way all day. You helped. You really helped a lot. I won't let you in tomorrow if you don't accept wages for your work."

Edward began to argue, but Naomi held up her hand.

"Remember, my daed's recovery lies on the condition of your presence here. So, think carefully before turning down this envelope again. I understand that you don't mind helping, and regardless if you enjoyed it or not, you deserve to be paid for your work. Accept it, please?"

Edward hesitated for a moment before he finally nodded. "Fine, I'll take it, but it really…"

"Isn't necessary," Naomi smiled. "Denke for today, Edward. I'll see you tomorrow morning."

Edward said goodbye before he set off for home. He didn't mind the long walk; it was refreshing to be outside after spending all day indoors. He had a smile on his face and a skip in his step the whole way home. Not only had he spent the day in the bakery, but he had an envelope of wages to show for it.

For the first time in his life, Edward felt like he was doing something right.

REALITY CAN BE HEARTBREAKING

*N*aomi hadn't seen her father in three days.

She had gone to see him the evening after he had the operation, but she had been hesitant to leave Edward alone in the bakery to go and see him during the day.

Over the last three days, all her fears concerning Edward had been eased. It was clear that although he had spent his life working in the fields of his family's farm, Edward was far from incapable when it came to a kitchen.

He had a natural way of helping the customers, making them feel welcome whilst serving them; and when it came to the kitchen part of the bakery, he was a welcome help.

So, this afternoon after the lunch rush, Naomi had asked Edward if he would be all right, taking care of the bakery until she returned, so that she could go and visit her father. Edward had insisted he'd be fine, which Naomi was certain would be the case, and yet it still felt strange leaving the bakery in someone's care that wasn't a Hostetler.

She knocked lightly on the door to her father's room before she pushed open the door. From the brief conversation she had with the nurse, her father was recovering very well after the operation. Although he wouldn't be released from the hospital for some time yet.

"Naomi, is something wrong?" Joseph sat up in bed, flinching with pain the moment Naomi stepped into the room.

"Nee, why would something be wrong?" Naomi asked, confused as she moved to her father's side.

"The bakery... have you closed it for the afternoon?" her father asked with concern in his voice.

Naomi smiled before she shrugged. "Nee, Edward is looking after the bakery and baking the last batch of scones for the day." A soft chuckle escaped her. "When you said I had to let him help, I was determined to put him in a corner and only summon him when I really had no other choice. But he's proven to be quite efficient in both the kitchen and the shop, Daed."

Relief washed over her father's face. "I'm so happy to hear that, although I'm not surprised. His mother had mentioned to me before at how much Edward enjoyed working in the kitchen."

"Really?" Naomi frowned curiously. "Well, he's surprised me more than once. When he isn't helping customers, he's baking or cleaning the kitchen. I didn't expect him to enjoy it. But he seems to."

"Have you been paying him?" Joseph asked.

"Jah, he insisted it wasn't necessary, but I told him it wasn't optional. He's actually working, not just being in my way. Now, enough about the bakery, Daed. How are you?" Naomi's eyes softened with empathy for her father. "I can imagine you're tired of being in bed."

Her father scoffed. "You guessed it. And when I am allowed out of bed, I must walk with a walker, like a toddler in a walking ring."

Naomi glanced towards the walker standing in the corner of her father's room. It was hard for her to see her father so vulnerable. He had always been a strong and independent man, and

Naomi understood that being dependent on nurses was very tough on him.

She couldn't help but think of the stairwell at home—would her father ever be able to climb it again? She pushed the thought aside and smiled at him. "At least it doesn't look as if you're in a lot of pain. Are they managing it?"

Her father nodded. "Jah, they give me something for the pain every few hours." A sigh escaped him as he glanced out the window with a faraway look. "I'm starting physical therapy on Monday."

"That sounds promising. I'm sure you're eager to start moving again, to get back to the bakery?" Naomi asked hopefully.

Her father was quiet for a short while before he answered. "Actually… I've been considering taking a less active role in the bakery for a while now. You're more than competent to manage it on your own, but I knew the work was too much. Perhaps… Edward is the answer."

Naomi frowned, confused for a moment. "You mean keep Edward on permanently? Daed, you shouldn't give up so quickly."

Joseph shook his head. "My dear dochder, you might be only twenty years old, but you forget your daed is nearing the wrong side of sixty. Your mamm and I were so blessed to have you, but we did have you late in life. The long hours have been getting to me for a while now. And having all this time to think, I've come to realize that I would like to have a garden again. I would like to sit on my porch and watch the sunset in my old age…."

"You want to move?" Naomi exclaimed, horrified. "The bakery is our home."

"The bakery is the home of the person who manages it," her father interrupted her. "I haven't decided anything just yet. I'm just voicing my thoughts. Perhaps this fall, and Edward, are both fated. All I'm saying is, keep an open mind, Naomi. The doctors have given me very realistic expectations for my recovery, and it might take a year before I'm back to my old self again. That's a long time..."

"I'm sure it won't take that long. You're active, fit, and stubborn. That must count for something."

Joseph smiled fondly at his daughter. "Of course, it counts. I'm just glad you have Edward there to help you while I can't. And he can't be that terrible if you feel comfortable leaving him in charge of the bakery to come and visit me?"

Naomi nodded. "He is a great help, I'll admit that. But we're not making any decisions today. Now, tell me if you've at least had any visitors?"

Naomi listened with half an ear as her father told her about the members of the community that had come to visit him. She listened to tales about the nurses—the kind and the stern ones—and even allowed him to complain about the food.

By the time she said goodbye, it was with a rather heavy heart.

It was time for her to realize that her father wasn't young anymore, and it didn't matter how much she believed in his recovery. His age did count against him. Perhaps she would be needing Edward's help longer than she imagined.

GUT SURPRISE – BAD SURPRISE

Working at the bakery had given Edward the confidence he needed to follow his brother's advice. Although he had so many thoughts on food and recipes, it felt good to know that his instincts had been right.

He was a more capable cook and baker than he had imagined.

After working in the bakery for the last ten days, he wanted the opportunity to cook a family dinner for his family. He wanted his father to be surprised by his talent and for once not scoff at Edward's love for doing a women's chores, as his father thought of it.

"I'm not sure about this, Edward." His mother was very hesitant when he asked her if he could cook.

"Mamm, please. I need a chance to prove to Daed what I can do. I've bought all the ingredients from my wages; all I need from you is to do is to keep an eye out for when Daed and Bram return from the fields," Edward all but pleaded.

He'd arranged to leave the bakery three hours earlier today, for just this purpose. He could understand that his mother didn't want to go against his father's wishes, but he needed her help.

Edwina glanced at the variety of ingredients on the kitchen table and let out a heavy sigh. "All right, I'll keep out an eye. But what if you're not done yet? I can't finish a meal I didn't start?"

Edward glanced at the clock on the wall. "They won't be back for at least another three hours. I'm sure I'll be done long before then."

His mother hesitated for another moment before she finally nodded. "Then you'd best get started. Do you need me to help you prepare the vegetables?"

Edward shook his head, feeling excitement build in his veins. "Nee, I just need you to take a seat, enjoy a cup of tea, and keep me company." He offered his mother a cup of tea before he set to work.

While he worked, he could see his mother's brows raise a couple of times at his flavor combinations, but she didn't once voice her doubt.

Edward stirred and boiled, tasted, and seasoned, and enjoyed every second of it. When Daisy returned from her babysitting job, she was baffled to find him in the kitchen. But a brief word from Edwina quickly brought Daisy up to speed on the plan.

Daisy set about setting the table, while complimenting the aromas emanating from the kitchen. Edward had just finished carving the ham when he saw his brother and his father approach the barn from the fields.

"All set," Edward said, feeling triumphant at the feast he had cooked.

"Edward, I'm sure if it tastes as gut as it smells, your daed would be very proud," Edwina assured him.

Edward's smile was filled with hope as he excused himself from the kitchen. Just as had been arranged, his mother pretended to be finishing dinner when his brother and father arrived.

"That smells wunderbaar, Edwina," Samuel praised his wife when he entered the kitchen.

"Then you'd better go wash up, so we can eat before it goes cold," she instructed him with a firm smile.

A short while later, the Fischer family was gathered at the table. Edward couldn't help but feel proud at the spread that weighed down the table. There was honey glazed ham, cilantro infused mashed potatoes, fried green beans with mushrooms, broccoli and cheese bake, baby carrots infused with aniseed and maple syrup, as well as a pumpkin bake.

Instead of the usual sweet pumpkin bake his mother made, Edward had fried bacon and onions before mixing them with the pumpkin and baking it with a layer of cheese.

It was everything his family was used to eating, just prepared in a slightly different way.

"Gutness, Edwina. Is there a special occasion we forgot about? You've served up a feast?" Samuel was clearly impressed once he had helped himself to everything on the table.

"Not at all. I just felt like cooking today, experimenting a little as well, I might add." Edwina smiled at her husband before glancing nervously at Edward.

Edward couldn't help but feel nervous as well. This was nothing like his mother's cooking. Perhaps he should've stuck to more traditional Amish recipes, instead of creating a completely original meal.

He glanced around the table as his family began to eat, quietly praying that they liked his food.

His mother was the first to compliment him, indirectly, of course. "These potatoes are amazing." She quickly smiled at his father. "I should definitely try making this again."

"The pumpkin is a gut surprise. You expect it to be sweet and spiced with cinnamon, but instead it's savory with bites of bacon. You can certainly make this again," Samuel praised his wife.

By the time everyone's plates were clear, most had already indulged in second helpings. Edward couldn't help but feel pleased. It was clear they enjoyed his meal. Now he just had to hope his father would be pleased at his talents and not angry because he had tricked him into eating it.

As if his mother read his mind, she turned to his father with a proud expression. "Samuel, I'm so glad you enjoyed supper, because I know you won't be angry when I tell you that I didn't cook it."

His father's brow furrowed as he turned to his mother. "Edwina, what do you mean you didn't cook it?"

"Edward cooked it. He bought all the ingredients with his wages and asked me to let you think I cooked it. He was afraid if you knew he cooked it, you would've been prejudiced before even tasting his creations. But it was wunderbaar, wasn't it Samuel?" Edwina turned to Edward with a proud smile. "Our seeh really has a true talent when it comes to the kitchen."

"Edward, did you really cook all this food?" Samuel asked, with a hint of doubt in his voice.

"Jah, Daed. I did. I'm glad you enjoyed it," Edward said humbly.

His father shook his head with a baffled expression. "Your mamm is right, Edward. The food was wunderbaar. Where did you learn how to cook like this?"

Edward shrugged. "Some of it from Mamm, the rest... I don't know, Daed. I guess it's like you when you look at a field and you know what it needs. I look at ingredients and know how they would taste together."

His father was far from looking at Edward with the same pride he had for Bram, but there was a flicker of hope in Edward's heart. He had surprised his father with his capabilities. Perhaps that was enough for now.

Edward couldn't be sure if his father was being kind because they hadn't seen much of each other since Edward had started at the bakery, or if it was because of the meal. But for the first time in months, his father didn't hackle him over dinner, instead without a single negative word for Edward wanting to do *women's chores*, he excused himself from the table.

It wasn't praise, but it wasn't criticism either.

In Edward's mind, that was a step in the right direction.

BRINGING FLAVOR TO LIFE

*I*t didn't matter how grateful Naomi was for Edward's help, the order in front of her was simply impossible to deliver.

A heavy sigh escaped her as she leaned over the myriad of recipe books.

"Something wrong?" Edward asked, walking into the kitchen.

It was almost a half hour before she expected him to arrive for work. Naomi had realized that Edward came in a little earlier every morning and stayed a little later every night. He didn't leave until everything had been done for the day. She appreciated his effort, but that wouldn't rescue the situation she had landed herself in.

"Jah," Naomi admitted with a sad smile. "Hullo Edward. You're very early."

Edward shrugged. "No use waiting around at home. Once my chores are done, I'd rather get here and get to work." He hung up his coat and joined her at the recipe books. "What's wrong?"

"A customer, one my daed usually helps, phoned in yesterday. They asked us to handle the catering for her husband's birthday. Of course, without hesitation, I agreed. Then this morning I referred to the catering order she placed last time, and... it's impossible."

"Why is it impossible?" Edward asked with a frown.

Naomi's tummy tilted strangely at his proximity. His eyes searched hers and she felt a little heat flush her cheeks. "Because... she's expecting the variety we offered her the last time. Without Daed here... I simply can't give her that. Baking has always been my specialty, and cooking Daed's. She wants the order to be seventy-five savory, and twenty-five sweet. I can't cook that number of savory dishes, even if I wanted to."

"Why not?" Edward repeated curiously.

Naomi let out a huff of frustration. "I'm not a gut cook. That's why! And I simply don't have the time. I'm just going to have to let her know that with Daed in the hospital, we won't be able to help her."

"And then she'll use someone else and next time she might not even phone you again," Edward pointed out the fact that Naomi had been trying to avoid.

"What other choice do I have?" Naomi asked, feeling hopeless.

"You can give me until the end of today. Let me see what I can do, and then you can decide," Edward suggested.

"What do you mean, what you can do?" Naomi asked with a hesitant frown.

Edward looked a little uncertain for a moment before he spoke. "Until I came to work at your bakery, I hadn't ever really cooked or baked before. I've been interested in it my entire life, but never had the opportunity. My daed would rather have me in the fields than in the kitchen. I have several recipes and ideas in my head, but since I haven't made them before, I want to test them first. If you like them, I can do the savory portion of the order."

Naomi frowned. "You mean you've never cooked or baked until a little more than a week ago?"

"Jah," Edward shrugged.

"But how are you so gut at it?" Naomi asked, baffled.

"I like it. It's always interested me. I would watch Mamm cook, sometimes I'd help Lucy, our neighbor, and then I'd think what I would've done differently."

"I'm not sure if that even makes sense, but I'll give you until the end of today," Naomi promised.

Naomi avoided Edward's section of the kitchen for the rest of the day. She didn't want to be prejudiced about his recipes or ideas before she tasted them. That's why when he began to wrap cherries and cheese in bacon, she headed to the front of the store.

The scents coming from the kitchen were mouth-watering, but Naomi waited patiently until Edward was ready for her to taste his creations.

By the time Naomi began to close the bakery, she couldn't help but be curious about the variety of savory dishes Edward had made. She moved into the kitchen and couldn't help but laugh at the way he had plated everything out on a platter, as if she were a client.

"Right, you can take a seat over there. I've poured you some apple juice to clear your palate between items." Edward gestured towards a seat.

Naomi noticed he was nervous. Judging by the way his savory snacks looked, she couldn't imagine why. "Am I finally allowed to taste?"

Edward nodded. "Let me explain to you what each item is. You said they want finger-friendly foods. With the previous order, I noticed your father made small savory pies, meatballs, chicken wings and a few other similar items. I thought I'd try something different, but if you don't like it, I can make the meatballs and chicken wings your father made for them."

Naomi chuckled. "I'm sure I'll like it. What's this?"

Naomi picked up the small bacon skewer with a frown.

"That is a bacon-wrapped cherry and cheese kebab. Then over

here you have the beef kebabs, marinated with soya sauce, and finished with a sweet and sour sauce. This is spinach and feta tartlets, with a dash of spring onion, and over here you have miniature cornbread muffins. It's my mother's recipe, but I added some cheese and inside there is a cream cheese surprise. Last, but not least, are the corn fritters. Once again, my mamm's recipe, but I added some dill to give it more flavor and seasoned it with paprika for depth."

Naomi's eyes widened with surprise. "Edward, that sounds... wunderbaar. It looks even better."

"Don't get too excited. Remember, most of these snacks I made today for the very first time."

Naomi shrugged; confident his snacks would taste amazing.

And she wasn't wrong. With every bite she took, she had the familiar comfort of ingredients she recognized, but at the same time her palate was dancing with the surprise of wonderful new flavor combinations. Everything was wonderful, but her personal favorite was the cornbread muffins. When you looked at them you expected a normal cornbread muffin, but as soon as you took a bite, the cream cheese exploded in your mouth.

"Edward, these muffins, the cream cheese–did you add something to it?"

"I knew it was too much. I minced some fried bacon with cilantro and used it to flavor the cream cheese," Edward admitted.

Naomi shook her head with bafflement. "It's the most wonderful flavors I've ever tasted. Usually, we just eat cornbread with jam, but this... Edward, this is amazing. It's my favorite item on this whole platter."

"Really?" Edward asked, surprised. "I wasn't expecting that. What did you think about the other items?"

Naomi laughed. "Edward, you have a gift. Truly. When it comes to the kitchen, I like to bake. I like to follow a recipe and knowing exactly what the results will be. Sure, I tweak a little here and there, but I never stray too far from what I know will work. Whereas this… you're brave enough to combine flavors I wouldn't even have imagined. And you have the talent to bring it all together. I think the customer is going to be overjoyed that you're responsible for the savory part of her order."

Edward's eyes widened. "You really trust me to do the entire savory part of the order?"

Naomi nodded. "Because you just proved you're the best mann for the job."

"Denke," Edward said sincerely. "For giving me a chance to make all of this. Denke for believing in me."

Naomi laughed as she moved towards Edward. "I didn't believe in you at all actually, I was just desperate. But I don't regret it at all." She tilted her head and searched his gaze. "I didn't want you to come and help at the bakery. I thought you were going to be in my way and of no help. I'm glad you proved me wrong, Edward. You're a great help."

Edward held her gaze and Naomi felt something inside her shift. Neither of them said a word, but for a few seconds it was as if the world had stopped spinning. Naomi was drawn to Edward in a way she'd never been drawn to a man ever before. It was both frightening and exciting.

Finally, Edward cleared his throat and stepped back. "I uhm… I packed a little of everything into this container. I thought you might like your daed to taste it as well."

Naomi, feeling slightly flushed, quickly nodded. "Denke, I was planning on going to see him tonight. I'm sure he'll be just as impressed as I am."

Edward said goodbye and left Naomi alone in the kitchen. For a moment, she just stood there wondering what had transpired between her and Edward. She might be twenty years old, but Naomi had never had a man look at her and feel as if her soul opened to him.

As if her heart wanted to reach out to him.

It was an unfamiliar feeling and yet one she couldn't wait to feel again.

A PERFECT COMBINATION

*I*t had been two weeks since Edward had begun working at the bakery.

Every single day, he felt a little more like he belonged, like he was finally walking through that door he had prayed for Gott to open. For so long, he had dreamed of finding an outlet for his talent, and now finally he had that opportunity.

The best part about exploring his love for cooking was getting to know Naomi. Edward admired everything about her. She was competent, an amazing baker, and she made Edward feel good about himself. When he was with her, he didn't feel ashamed to express his love for cooking. He wasn't cautious about voicing ideas about flavor combinations, or even just being himself.

It was the first time in his life that Edward could just be the person he really was. He didn't have to hide away a part of himself or try to pretend to love something he wasn't passionate about.

Regardless of the bakery being closed or it being a Saturday afternoon, Edward was happy to be at the bakery. The catering order would be collected in two hours, and together he and Naomi were putting the final touches on the platters.

"I wish Daed could see this. He would be so impressed with us," Naomi said as she wiped the edge of the sweet platters. She had dusted a little icing sugar over the top to make it look even more attractive than it already was.

Edward smiled at her as he arranged the items on his platters. "Your daed would've been very impressed with you, especially."

Naomi's platters were truly phenomenal. She had basically made every single pastry and sweet treat they offered in the bakery on a miniature scale. There were tiny chocolate cakes, eclairs, custard slices, and even tiny apple pies.

"Denke Edward, but you outdid yourself as well." Naomi glanced over at his platters. "I just hope the kebabs will taste all right without the sauce."

Edward frowned. He checked the platters to make sure every kebab had been dunked in the sweet and sour sauce before turning to Naomi with a questioning look.

Naomi moved towards him with a curious smile before she reached up and dabbed away something on his cheek. "That sauce..."

Edward chuckled. "I tasted it to make sure it was right."

"I know," Naomi laughed. She stood back and admired their work. "It looks like we catered for a family of very small people."

Edward joined in with the laughter. "You mean a whole community of very small people?"

"Today didn't feel like work at all," Naomi mused, almost to herself.

Edward nodded. "It didn't."

Throughout the day, they had bantered and laughed as they worked. Edward had teased Naomi about decorating each minia-ture chocolate cake as if it were for a wedding. When Edward had used a large syringe to insert the cream cheese into the corn-bread muffins, Naomi had teased him about inoculating the cornbread.

It had been one of the best days of Edward's life. Regardless of his father's opinion, Edward knew without a single doubt in his mind that this was what he wanted to do for the rest of his life. He didn't have the same passion for farming as his father and his brother, but he did have a passion for cooking.

Looking at everything he had created, and knowing how it would be enjoyed, Edward couldn't help but feel as if he had just proved to himself that he didn't just have a dream. It was a dream he could achieve.

He searched Naomi's eyes and wondered if the way he felt when he was around her was just about cooking, or if it was because of Naomi.

For a moment, he was taken back to last summer when he thought he'd been in love with Lucy. Of course, he had enjoyed Lucy's company, but had he ever felt this way with Lucy?

Edward was caught off guard for a moment, realizing that he didn't just appreciate Naomi's company, he liked her.

"Edward, is something the matter?" Naomi asked, sensing his change of demeanor.

Edward quickly shook his head and summoned a smile. "Nee, everything is just perfect."

There was a knock on the door of the bakery since Naomi had locked the doors hours ago. Saved by the knock, Edward thought gratefully as Naomi rushed to let in the customer who had ordered the platters.

Alone for a few seconds, Edward knew this was something he would ponder on later. Perhaps he hadn't only been led to the bakery by fate to explore his talent, perhaps there was more here to explore than just cooking and baking.

UNEXPECTED JEALOUSY

"The physical therapy is going better than expected, but the doctor is still cautious because of my daed's age," Naomi explained to Edward when she returned from visiting her father. "Although it's been more than two weeks, the doctor insists on keeping my daed for a few more days."

"I'm sorry to hear that," Edward sympathized as he restocked the pastry display. "I knew you were looking forward to having him home."

"Then there's that, as well," Naomi sighed as she fastened her apron that read Hostetler Bakery around her waist. "The doctor said he didn't' want Daed to climb stairs for at least another few months. He wants to limit the mobility of his hip until he is certain both the hip and Daed are strong enough before he starts climbing stairs daily."

"Ach nee," Edward turned to her with an expression of concern. "What are you going to do?"

"I don't know. I guess I could ask my aunt if he could stay with her in the community until he's better, but I know he won't like that." Naomi glanced towards the office in the back. "I thought perhaps I could move some of the shelves out of the office and put his bed in there temporarily. The office is big enough and we have space in the kitchen for the shelves… but it's going to be a lot of work."

"That sounds like a gut plan. I can help. I'm sure your daed will be more comfortable recuperating here than in your aunt's home," Edward offered. "Ask him, and if he agrees, I'll help you move everything so that it's ready when he's discharged."

"Denke, Edward." Naomi smiled at him in a way that made his heart lift. "Besides, if he's here, he'll at least feel useful again. He hates not being able to work."

Edward nodded. "If a man spends most of his life working, idle time is a curse, not a blessing."

Naomi laughed. "You sound just like my daed."

The bells jingled on the door, and Edward glanced up to see Lucy walking into the bakery. A smile curved his mouth. "Lucy, what a gut surprise."

Lucy returned his smile. "Hullo Edward. Jah, I finished my marketing in town and thought I'd stop by. Do you have time for kaffe?"

Edward glanced at Naomi, who quickly nodded in agreement, since it was quiet. "Of course. Would you like one of Naomi's pastries with that kaffe? She makes the best croissants. You have to try the dark chocolate and blackberry croissants."

Lucy laughed. "You've persuaded me."

Armed with coffee for them both and a croissant for Lucy, Edward joined her at one of the tables. "I promise you've never tasted anything like this."

Lucy took a bite of the croissant and softly moaned with pleasure. "Edward, you're right, this is wunderbaar."

"I know. All her pastries are." Edward smiled proudly at Naomi, who was standing only a few feet away.

He noticed her blush lightly before she disappeared into the kitchen.

"It's nice to see you again. I'm so used to seeing you around the farm. I've missed you these last few weeks." Lucy smiled at Edward as she reached for her coffee.

"I know. I've missed you as well. How are the plans for the wedding coming along?"

"Ach, you know. It's a wedding. Between my mamm and your mamm, I hardly have any choices to make. I think they've invited the entire community, along with relatives from all over the country. My mamm has probably sewed my dress five times by now, insisting every time that it isn't just right. And then there's the food. Although they agree on absolutely everything, they keep arguing about the food. My mamm insists her pies are the best, while your mamm insists hers are. I swear, before Bram and I say our vows, a war is going to break out between our mothers," Lucy finished with a sigh.

Edward chuckled. "You know mothers. They only want what is best. Sometimes that can be more than a little overwhelming."

"Right now, I'd be happy with saying my vows during a regular Sunday church service and having sandwiches for the reception." Lucy chuckled. "Enough about me and my complaints. How are you? Bram says you seem happy?"

Edward couldn't stop the smile from spreading across his face. "I am. I am very happy. I always thought this was what I was meant to do, but to be actually doing it…. Is it wrong of me to love working in this bakery more than I've ever loved working on the farm?"

"Nee, not at all," Lucy assured him. "Has your daed come to terms with it yet?"

Edward shrugged. "I'm not sure. He hasn't made any degrading comments recently, but he is still very distant with me. Lucy… I can't help but feel that this is what I want to do, whether he approves or not."

"I can imagine it would be very hard for you to pursue your dreams without your daed's blessings, knowing how much it matters to you, but you must do what makes you happy, Edward.

Just remember that. Do you remember how miserable you were last year at this time? Your crop was a disaster, and you felt like a failure? Have you felt like that here?"

Edward quickly shook his head. "Not once. Sure, I've made mistakes, flops of course, but every time I do, I realize what I did wrong to change it the next time. It's... it's what I was meant to do."

Lucy reached across the table for Edward's hand and squeezed it tightly as she smiled at him. "I've never seen you this happy, Edward. It makes my heart warm to see you like this."

Edward laughed. "Denke, and for your support all these years. If it hadn't been for you... I might have given up on my dreams a long time ago."

"That's what friends are for. How much longer are you going to help here?" Lucy asked, glancing around the bakery.

"I'm not sure. Mr. Hostetler is being discharged from the hospital next week, but he won't be able to work yet. Besides, while I'm helping here, I'm saving up. Hopefully, I can save enough to start something on my own. Perhaps catering, or even that farm stall I've always dreamed about."

Lucy's smile broadened. "That's a wunderbaar idea. Just remember, if your daed is stubborn about having a farm stall on his land, we'll ask mine."

It was nice to catch up with Lucy again. By the time she left, Edward had thoroughly enjoyed seeing her. He appreciated her friendship and was more than grateful that she would soon be his sister-in-law.

He found Naomi in the kitchen, rolling out pastry dough. "Need some help?"

"Nee, I'm fine." Naomi pressed down the rolling pin before rolling over the sheet of dough again. "It was nice of your sweet-heart to stop by. She seems sweet. You two make a great couple."

Edward frowned, first at Naomi's strange use of the word 'nice' and then at her strange tone of voice. It took him a minute to catch on before a smile tilted the corners of his mouth. Was she jealous?

"It was nice of you to let me spend some time with her," Edward replied sweetly.

When Naomi didn't look up, he knew his assessment had been spot on. Laughter bubbled from his throat as he snatched the rolling pin from her hands. Naomi looked up with an irritable look. "Give that back."

Edward held it up in the air, knowing he was irritating her. "Lucy is very nice. And it was very nice of her to stop by. And jah, we have a nice *friendship*, since she's engaged to be married to my bruder."

Naomi's eyes widened before her cheeks flushed bright red. "She's not your sweetheart?"

Edward laughed. "Nee. Why? Would it have bothered you if she was?"

Edward had never flirted with a girl before, and he had a feeling he was toeing that line right now. Naomi's cheeks reddened even more.

"Don't be ridiculous. Why would it bother me?" Naomi snapped.

Edward couldn't help but feel hope expand in his chest at her short answer as he handed her the rolling pin. Perhaps he wasn't the only one experiencing unexpected feelings.

Just perhaps, Naomi liked him for more than just his skills in the kitchen.

Knowing it was much too soon to explore whatever feelings he had for her, he let the subject go. But deep down, he couldn't help but hope that perhaps Naomi had feelings for him as well.

TIME FOR A CHANGE

*N*aomi stood behind her father, knowing she would only relax once he was off his feet.

He had been discharged from the hospital this morning, and after a last session of physical therapy, Naomi had arranged for a driver to bring her father home. With every step he took from the car to the bakery door, Naomi had caught herself holding her breath.

Although her father seemed quite capable of walking with the walker, Naomi still couldn't help but fear that he would fall. Edward had offered to help him over the threshold of the bakery door, but her father had stubbornly refused.

The short distance from the door of the bakery to the office had felt to Naomi as if it was ten miles long. Her father walked slowly, taking extra care with every step. When he finally reached the office, she allowed herself to let go the breath she had been holding.

"Naomi, you didn't have to go through so much trouble. I would've been fine sleeping along the shelves and the filing cabinets," Joseph turned to her with a grateful look.

"Edward helped. We wanted to make it as comfortable for you as possible." Naomi glanced around the once cluttered office and approved of what she and Edward had achieved.

All the filing cabinets and shelves had been moved into the corner of the kitchen. Instead of the cluttered office that doubled as a storage space, Naomi realized how large the space was. With only the desk for her father to work at in the corner, there had been enough space for Naomi and Edward to make it homey for her father.

His favorite chair now stood in one corner, with another chair for a visitor or a friend. The bed was against the wall, with a bedside table and a lamp within her father's reach whenever he was lying down.

A chest of drawers had been brought down from upstairs for his clothes, along with a few other items he had in his room. It no longer looked like the office of a busy bakery, but instead like the welcoming room of a frail patient recovering after a major operation.

"How kind of you. It's truly wunderbaar. Much different from I remember. I never knew it was this big," Joseph said, making his way to the chair.

Naomi stood close by as her father gently lowered himself into the chair. Once she was certain he was comfortable, she took a seat on the chair beside him. "I know. I was surprised as well. We moved around the kitchen a little to accommodate the shelves and filing cabinets, but it works perfectly. Edward had the idea of creating a savory side and a pastry side in the kitchen, with the pantry to reflect each side. It works wonderfully. And the storage area at the back of the kitchen has been repacked, clearing up enough space for all the extra things we had stored in here."

"Seems to me Edward has been quite some help around here?" Joseph asked with a cocked brow.

"He has. After the catering order was delivered, we've received another two. Business is really doing well, so I don't want you to worry about that at all. Edward is handling all the savory items and I'm handling the baking. We make a surprisingly gut team," Naomi admitted with a smile.

Her father nodded, pleased. "With business doing so gut, Naomi, I've been thinking we should offer Edward a permanent position. It's clear he's more than capable and you yourself just said what a gut team you make. I'm not sure if I'll ever be able to handle the physical pace of the bakery again. This way, I don't have to be concerned that you're overwhelmed and when I feel up to it, I can help."

Naomi smiled at her father, glad that he'd made the suggestion. She had been thinking about it but didn't want to suggest it and make her father think that he was no longer welcome in his own bakery. Having the suggestion come from him was the perfect solution. "I agree, Daed. He's a real asset to the bakery and the customers get along with him very well. I've also thought that if we offer him a permanent position, that we should increase his wages. He's proved that he's worth much more than we're paying him now."

Joseph nodded in agreement. Naomi and her father discussed how much they would offer him and what his duties would be before Naomi left her father to rest. She found Edward in the kitchen, sliding a batch of muffins into the oven.

"And is he all settled?" Edward asked, noticing her.

"Jah. You didn't have to bake the muffins; I was on my way." Naomi smiled at him gratefully.

Edward shrugged. "I had time. What does he think of his office room?"

Naomi laughed. "He loves it."

"That's gut." Edward smiled at her in a way that made her head spin just a little.

"Edward, do you mind if we talk for a moment? There is

something I'd like to discuss with you," Naomi asked, crossing her fingers behind her back. She had picked up that Edward's father wasn't very fond of his love for the kitchen, but she hoped that wouldn't affect Edward's decision when she made him the offer.

"Of course, but first, let me make us some kaffe."

TRADITION CAN BE A FOOLISH FIEND

*E*dward couldn't wait to get home.

He wanted to tell his parents about the amazing job offer Naomi had made him, and the good salary he expected to receive. He was more than a little excited to have his dreams fall into place. And with a permanent position at the bakery, that meant he could spend more time with Naomi.

Over the last few weeks, he had come to fall for Naomi a little more every day. But since she was not only his boss but someone who clearly had never been interested in courting before, Edward wanted to take his time pursuing his feelings for her.

The last thing he wanted was to scare Naomi away by admitting his feelings for her too soon. He didn't know how to express it, but he felt as if his future lay with Naomi and the Hostetler bakery. He wasn't sure exactly how or when, but he couldn't help but feel excited at what the future had in store for him.

Edward was all but bursting with excitement by the time his family was gathered around the kitchen table. Lucy was joining them for dinner tonight, and Edward knew she would be just as excited at the opportunity as he was.

He glanced across the table towards his father and couldn't

help but feel a knot of anxiety form in his belly. His father might have approved of him working in the bakery, or rather helping for now, but would he approve of Edward dedicating his life to cooking?

The dinner conversation ran back and forth around the farm. It was planting season and Bram was ahead of schedule with most of his fields. He had taken the risk of planting a few other crops as well, hoping his risk would pay off.

What was wonderful for Edward was to see how his father approved of the risks Bram was taking. Risks that would influence the livelihood of their whole family. It only proved how much his father trusted Bram to run the farm.

Edward waited until there was a lull in the conversation before he took his chance. "I have some gut news," Edward announced with a smile.

"Well then," Edwina said with a smile, "let's hear it."

Edward smiled at his mother before he began to speak. "Naomi and Joseph Hostetler made me an offer today. They want me to be the savory bakery manager. The hours will remain the same, but I will be responsible for all the savory items that the bakery makes, as well as helping with deciding what is on offer in the bakery itself. I will have full power over the savory menu." Edward couldn't help but feel his face split in two with joy as he voiced the words. "And above that, they are offering me a significant increase in wages. Joseph wants to take a less active role in the bakery, and with me and Naomi making such a gut team, he wants me there permanently."

"Edward, that is wunderbaar. You've really proven yourself to be an asset then," Daisy praised him with a broad smile.

"I am happy for you, bruder. It's clear they appreciate your capabilities." Bram nodded at him with pride in his eyes.

"That's quite a bit of responsibility. You must have proved yourself to Joseph for him to be willing to give you such a position. And the increase in wages...it's gut for a mann to be able to support his familye one day," Edwina praised her son with a look of pride and an affectionate smile.

Samuel's fist slammed against the table, bringing everyone to complete silence. Edward noticed Lucy's eyes almost doubling with fright before he met his father's angry gaze.

"Listen to all of you, praising him for being able to do a woman's job. Do you hear me priding myself in the fact that Daisy can feed the chickens? It's preposterous. It's one thing for Joseph Hostetler to spend his whole life in the kitchen—he didn't have another choice, because that is all his daed taught him, but you are a different matter altogether," Samuel cried out with agitation. "I taught you how to farm, how to work the fields, and how to read the seasons. But instead, you want to spend your life up to your arms in dough. It's a woman's job, Edward. I never should've agreed to helping the Hostetler's in the first place."

"Samuel, please, be reasonable…" Edwina began to plead with her husband, but one firm look made her keep her silence.

"I will not allow this. You hear me, Edward? You will turn down that offer tomorrow. No son of mine will spend his life in a bakery. As soon as Joseph is fit to take his place again, you'll be back on the farm. It's time you paid attention to your heritage and learned to farm like your bruder. How can your sons be proud of you one day for cooking? There is no pride in that, not for a mann!"

Edward wished the floor would swallow him whole. If he had thought that cooking for his father had made any difference in his opinion of a man in the kitchen, he had been wrong. It was clear to Edward now that his father would never approve of his love for cooking.

It didn't matter how hard he tried to prove himself. Unless he was a farmer like Bram, his father would never be proud of him.

Edward opened his mouth to argue, to remind his father of how many Amish bakers there were around the world, but before he could even attempt to redeem himself, his father left the table.

His father walked out of the house, slamming the door behind him.

Edward couldn't bear the sympathetic looks aimed at him from around the table. It didn't matter how sorry anyone felt for him, it was clear his father would never let him strive for his dreams.

Because his dreams belonged to a woman, not to mann.

"I'll turn down the offer in the morning," Edward mumbled before he excused himself from the table.

What other choice did he have?

BITTERSWEET TRIUMPH

*T*urning down Naomi's offer had been the hardest thing Edward had ever had to do. He had been given the opportunity of his dreams and instead of accepting it with open arms; he had slammed the door in opportunity's face.

He couldn't help but feel frustrated with his father for making him do it.

But today wasn't a day for frustration, anger, or even arguments. Because today it was Bram and Lucy's wedding. A smile curved the corners of Edward's mouth. He was ecstatic that his best friend and his brother would say their vows to each other today. He knew they would take good care of each other, and that Gott would bless them with a beautiful marriage.

Before he could start thinking about this afternoon's wedding, he still had a few things to do at the bakery. They had received another large catering order earlier this week. Edward and Naomi had worked hard for the last few days to complete the order and as Edward plated the last of the savory items, he couldn't help but feel a bittersweet pride wash over him.

He so enjoyed working at the bakery, but as soon as Joseph was back on his feet, Edward would be back in the fields.

Was it wrong of him to want Joseph's recuperation to take a little longer?

Edward pushed the horrible thought from his mind as he began sealing the platters with lids.

"All done?" Naomi asked as she looked at his platters.

"All done." Edward stood back and took off his apron. "I hope the customer is happy. I have got to go, or I'll be late to my own bruder's wedding."

Naomi nodded. "I'll see you there."

Her comment didn't shock Edward in the least. His mother had invited almost the *entire* community.

Later that afternoon when the ceremony came to an end, and the bishop announced Lucy and Bram mann and frau, Edward couldn't help but be overjoyed. As his brother and his new wife stood in front of the congregation, Edward hoped that one day he could feel that same overwhelming joy that shone on his brother's face.

He glanced across the aisle to where the women and young girls sat and spotted Naomi in the crowd. Hope swelled in chest, as he dreamed of a future with Naomi.

Edward pushed the thought aside, knowing that Naomi's life was the bakery. With his father's disapproval of Edward's love for cooking, he simply couldn't imagine a future with Naomi.

Feeling a little down, Edward followed everyone outside to where the tables were laden with food. As he neared the tables, a frown creased his brow. He recognized his own creations and that of Naomi, as he moved from one table to the next. Had he been so occupied with the bakery that he hadn't even realized they were catering for his brother's wedding?

He caught sight of Naomi and smiled at her across the table. He wasn't sure if she meant to keep it from him, or if it simply slipped her mind. Or perhaps she had simply thought he knew.

As the guests, most of whom Edward had known his whole life, began to fuss over the extraordinary food, Edward felt the rush of triumph. His father might not appreciate his talent, but at least there were those who did.

A HOLLOW VICTORY

*N*aomi felt her heart swell at the sight of Edward, but she quickly turned away.

When he had turned down her offer of a permanent position, she had truly believed that he would jump at the opportunity. But instead, he had made it clear that he would only be helping until her father was back on both feet.

Naomi wasn't sure if she was more disappointed because it meant her father's recovery now determined her time with Edward, or if it was because she wouldn't see Edward when her father was fully recovered.

Over the last few weeks, Naomi had allowed her heart to fall just a bit. She had never put much thought into courtship or finding a husband, but meeting Edward had changed all of that. Of course, in the distant future, she had dreamed of having a family, but those dreams had never really solidified until she met someone she could see herself spending her future with.

And that person was Edward.

There had been a few times over the last six weeks when she had been certain Edward felt the same way, but now she wasn't so sure. Surely, if he felt anything for her at all, he would've been eager for a chance to spend more time with her.

Instead, it seemed as if the thought had repulsed him. Why else would he have turned down her offer so easily?

Naomi pushed the thoughts of Edward aside. They only hurt more today because she had just witnessed a wedding. She couldn't help but feel as if she had been cheated out of her happiness, out of her chance at finding true love, now that she knew how eager Edward was to return to the fields.

The worst part was, it would be such a waste of his talent.

She had never met someone who had such an instinctive touch when it came to cooking. Edward didn't follow recipes like she did when she baked, instead, he created his own. Not only would his absence be felt at the bakery, but his creativity would be dearly missed. She began gathering the platters that were already empty, to set them aside, when a man approached her.

Naomi didn't recognize him at all. Since she and her father lived in town, she only saw the community at Sunday Service. As they were such a large community, it was impossible to know everyone.

"Are you the lady responsible for the catering?" the man asked her with a curious look.

Naomi nodded. "Jah, I am. I hope it was to your liking?"

The man chuckled and shook his head. "To my liking? It was wunderbaar. When my frau said she had decided to have the wedding catered, I thought it would be an unnecessary waste of money, but I can honestly say she didn't waste a single dime. The food was truly magnificent."

"Denke," Naomi smiled, enjoying the praise.

"I have yet to taste the pastries and those tiny cakes, but the savory tarts, quiches, and those beef kebabs... I've never tasted anything as gut in my entire life," the man emphasized with a nod.

Naomi nodded. "Then you should actually be thanking him,"

Naomi nodded towards Edward. "I only baked the confectionary items; Edward Fischer is responsible for all the savory items. He's a true talent when it comes to cooking."

The man's eyes widened with surprise. Naomi knew it was because Edward was a man; their community still had a very traditional outlook on who should be responsible for cooking.

"Wait, let me call him over, then you can thank him yourself." Naomi smiled at the man before she gestured Edward to come closer. "Edward, could you come here for a second?"

Perhaps if Edward knew how much people enjoyed his food, he might change his mind about accepting her offer.

Or at least, Naomi could hope.

CREDIT WHERE CREDIT IS DUE

The moment Edward noticed Naomi talking to his father, an anxious knot began to coil in his belly. He watched from across the table as his father smiled at something Naomi said, wondering why his father couldn't be that way with him.

When Naomi called him, Edward wasn't sure if he should run, hide, or simply join them. Finally, he knew it would be cowardly to run from his own father and the girl he had fallen in love with. He slowly made his way around the table, silently praying that his father wouldn't insult him in front of Naomi.

He knew what his father thought about his love of cooking. He didn't need his father to remind him of that. Especially not in front of the girl Edward hoped to court one day.

"Edward, denke for joining us. This man was just telling me that he's never had such wonderful food in his life. Especially your tartlets, quiches, and the beef kebabs," Naomi gushed.

Edward glanced at his father, unsure of what was happening, when he realized Naomi didn't know it was his father.

"Surely you made them from a recipe this lovely young lady gave you?"

Although his father was smiling, Edward could read the insult in his eyes. He didn't think Edward could create anything of value when it came to cooking.

Naomi's bubbly laughter filled the air before Edward could answer. "You think these are my recipes? I'm sorry, sir, but I'll have to disappoint you. My talents reach towards the sweeter end of the kitchen. Every single savory item that has been served here today, are Edward's original recipes. Every single one of them he created and perfected without any input from me. He's a true talent in the kitchen, just like I told you before."

Edward gulped past the fear closing in his throat. He knew that it was only a matter of time before his father would insult him.

But instead, his father surprised him when his brow began to furrow. "Is she telling the truth? Did you really make all of this? From your own recipes?" His father's voice now held cautious curiosity as he searched Edward's gaze.

Edward nodded. "Jah. The cornbread with the cream cheese filling is one of Mamm's recipes I adjusted."

"Here you are, Samuel. I've been looking all over for you. Naomi, it's so gut to see you. I must compliment you on the food." Edward's mother joined the conversation, completely oblivious to what was going on. "Do you still think hiring a caterer is a waste of money?"

Samuel shook his head, glancing at Edward with a baffled look. "Nee, I was just telling the caterer that the food is simply wunderbaar."

Edward stood glued to the spot, unsure what is father's next words would be. He glanced at Naomi and realized she had yet to catch on that these were his parents.

"I'm sorry. I'm slightly confused. Mrs. Maas placed the order, the bride's mamm. Do you have any relation to her?" Naomi asked with a frown.

A FATHER-SON REVELATION

*N*aomi watched Edward glance at the man and the woman before he turned to her with a hesitant look. "Naomi, please meet my parents. Samuel and Edwina Fischer."

Naomi's eyes widened with surprise. "Ach, now I understand. You're the groom's parents. I forgot for a moment that Bram is Edward's twin. Although I must admit, I didn't realize how alike they were. Denke again for allowing us to do the catering. I'm sure Edward must have had something to do with it."

"On the contrary…" Samuel said, glancing at Edward with a strange look.

"Actually, it was me and Lucy's mamm that couldn't come to an agreement. We kept arguing over whose dishes would be the best and finally, we just decided to have you cater for the wedding. That way we didn't have to spend days in the kitchen, and we knew the food would be wunderbaar. Lucy's mamm told me about the wonderful platters you have been making recently and I thought it was a gut idea," Edwina admitted.

"Why didn't you tell me that the catering was being done by the bakery where Edward worked?" Samuel asked a little defiantly.

Naomi wasn't sure why there was tension in the air. Especially between Edward and his father. Surely, if your son was such a talent in the kitchen, it was something to be proud of. Instead, the moment he had learned Edward was responsible for the savory snacks, he seemed caught off guard.

Edwina put her hands on her hips and turned to her husband with a narrowed look. "Because if I did, you would've refused just because it meant Edward would be in a kitchen. Look at all these guests Samuel. Every single one of them has complimented the food. Do you still think it's wrong for your seeh to work in a kitchen? He's gut at it, Samuel, and he enjoys it. Denying him of that would be like forcing you to sell your land. Imagine never digging your hands into the dirt again, Samuel. It would be a terrible thing to do."

Naomi glanced at Samuel and suddenly realized why Edward had turned down her offer. From what she could glean, it was clear that Edward's father didn't approve of his love for cooking. She couldn't imagine why. Gott blessed everyone with their own talents. Surely talent should be embraced and not judged.

Samuel let out a heavy sigh and turned to Edward with a curious look. "I never realized…. I simply thought you wanted to work in a kitchen because you were too lazy to work the fields. But now that I've seen what you can do…"

"Lazy?" Naomi cut in, regardless of whether if it was appropriate or not. "As someone who has spent my entire life working in a bakery, I just want to put in that there isn't time for laziness in a kitchen. Edward spends almost every minute of his day on his feet. How is that lazy?"

Samuel shook his head with an apologetic look. "Like I said, I didn't realize. It's clear to me now that not only do you enjoy cooking, but you're gut at it. It's like your mamm says, Edward, it would be wrong of me to keep you from doing what you're meant to do."

Edward gasped with surprise. Naomi looked from Samuel to

Edward and frowned. "Did you turn down the job offer because your daed wouldn't approve of you working in a kitchen?"

Before Edward could answer, Samuel did. "I apologize, Naomi, I was prejudiced against a son of mine spending his days in the kitchen like a frau. I was wrong, I admit it. I forbid Edward to accept the position you offered him. Edward, could you forgive me?" Samuel asked Edward with a hopeful look.

"Does that mean he has your blessing to accept my offer?" Naomi asked hopefully.

Samuel nodded, keeping his gaze on Edward. "Not only does he have my blessing to accept it, but I will also be proud if he does. Edward?"

Naomi could see how shocked Edward was by his father's change of heart. A smile curved the corners of her mouth as her future began to shine brightly again. "Edward? Do you accept the offer Daed and I made you?"

Edward let out a sigh before his face nearly split in two. "Of course, I accept it. Nothing would give me more joy than to have a permanent position at the bakery." He turned to his father and shook his head with baffled amazement. "Denke Daed, denke for being proud of me."

The look that passed between father and son was one that Naomi would never forget. Even for her, a stranger in their family, it was clear that they had just reached a new height in their relationship.

Samuel nodded. "It was wrong of me not to see you for who you were earlier."

"Samuel, kumm. The bishop is calling is," Edwina said before smiling at Naomi. "Probably to compliment us on the food."

A RUSH OF COURAGE

*E*dward watched his parents walk away, struggling to fathom what had just happened. A few moments ago, he was prepared to bid his dreams of the bakery and a future with Naomi goodbye, and now the fates had aligned in his favor.

He couldn't be sure, but he had a feeling that his mother and Lucy's mother didn't argue over the food at all. Somehow, he just knew that his mother had cleverly manipulated the situation, so that his father would be privy to what Edward could do. That he would have no choice but to see the magnitude of Edward's talents, and to be proud of his son.

By arranging that the bakery catered to his brother's wedding, not only did his father have a chance to taste Edward's creations, but he was surrounded by neighbors, friends, and family that complimented him on his son's talent.

Edward knew he would forever be grateful to his mother for what she did today.

"I had no idea that your daed didn't approve of your cooking?" Naomi said once his parents were out of earshot.

Edward nodded. "He compared my love for cooking to a man too lazy to do a man's chores and instead preferred the homely chores of a woman. He made it clear he would never approve of me working in a kitchen… until now."

"It's clear he is very proud of you today; you must be very happy."

"I am." Edward turned to her with a curious look. "Did you really not know we were catering for my bruder's wedding?"

"Not when the order was placed, nee. Mrs. Maas placed the order, so I thought nothing of it, and when I realized a few days ago that it was probably your bruder's wedding, I thought you'd convinced them to make use of the bakery," Naomi chuckled. "Seems we were both a little misled."

"Seems that way," Edward smiled. "I still can't believe my daed approves of me taking the position at the bakery. A permanent position. It feels as if one of my biggest dreams has just been realized."

"That's wunderbaar Edward." Naomi smiled at him in that way that made him dream of the future.

"Kumm, let me introduce you to my bruder and his bride," Edward said before he led her to Lucy and Bram.

"I've seen them before, but I don't really know them. You and your bruder are truly cut from the same cloth. It's only your eyes that are different," Naomi commented as they neared Bram and Lucy.

Edward nodded. "Jah. Our eyes and every facet of our personalities. Bram's entire future lies with the farm. He's building a haus there for him and Lucy as well. When it comes to farming, he takes after my daed and all the Fischer men that came before him. Whereas I… well, farming has never been my strong suit. Remind me one day to tell you about the time my daed gave me and my bruder each a field to test our abilities."

"Oh, he did?" Naomi asked curiously. "How did that go?"

Edward laughed; it was easy to laugh about his lack of farming skills now that he had found his true passion. "Let's just say it was a gut thing Daed only gave me one field."

Naomi laughed as they joined Bram and Lucy.

"Bram, Lucy, I'd like you to meet Naomi Hostetler. She's the woman responsible for running the bakery and as of today my new permanent employer," Edward said, feeling his shoulders broaden with pride.

Lucy's eyes widened with joy. "Really? Your daed gave you, his blessing?"

Naomi nodded eagerly. "He did. Edward is officially the manager of everything savory that comes out of Hostetler's Bakery."

"That's wunderbaar, bruder!" Bram said, slapping his brother on the back.

"Ach, I'm sorry Naomi, it's very gut to meet you. Edward has told us so much about you." Lucy turned to Naomi with a smile.

"Likewise," Bram agreed. "My bruder has been happier than I've ever seen him since he began working at the bakery."

"I'm happy to hear that. He's a true asset to the bakery. We're glad to have him." Naomi smiled at Edward before turning to the happy couple. "Congratulations once again. Gott's blessings on your marriage."

"Denke," Lucy accepted with a warm smile. "Bram, kumm, I see your aunt from Ohio wants to speak to us."

Bram and Lucy headed towards a distant aunt, leaving Edward and Naomi on their own. Edward glanced towards the tables, pleased to see that everyone was enjoying the food. "I'm sure we're going to get a lot more catering orders from the community. It isn't like the Amish to outsource catering, but just perhaps today changed that for the better."

Naomi nodded with excitement. "I can see having you on board is going to grow the bakery to new heights. I just wish my daed could've been here to see how much everyone is enjoying the food."

"You'll tell him tonight," Edward promised. "He's recovering well, but it's better he takes it slow than overextend himself and get injured again."

"I know," Naomi nodded.

For a moment, silence hung over them before Naomi turned to him with a curious look. Edward smiled before she even had a chance to speak. She was the most sincere, honest, loyal, kind, and creative person he'd ever met before. In time, he would gather enough courage to tell her how he really felt about her.

"Edward?" Naomi began. "You said earlier that accepting the position at the bakery realized one of your biggest dreams. What other big dreams do you have?"

"You mean other than cooking for life?" Edward teased.

"Jah?" Naomi asked with a look of intrigue.

Edward's heart skipped a beat. Was he ready to confess his feelings for her? Was he ready to tell her his dreams of the future involved her? He searched her eyes and felt hope swell in his chest. Today had brought him nothing but good luck. Perhaps he didn't have to wait to gather enough courage.

Perhaps he should take the feelings of triumph and joy and just be honest with Naomi about his other dreams for the future. He smiled into her eyes before he gathered the courage to speak.

"I have a few other dreams. Dreams of having a familye one day, dreams of perhaps opening a farm stall, but the biggest dream I have yet to achieve is to gather enough courage to ask you on a buggy ride. But I'm not sure when that will be," Edward shrugged as if he hadn't just revealed his intentions to court Naomi to her.

Naomi's eyes widened with a surprise before a smile curved the corners of her mouth. "It's a shame you don't have enough courage to ask me today. I might have just said jah."

Edward's smile broadened as he held her gaze. "I suddenly feel a rush of courage coming over me." He drew in a deep breath. "Naomi Hostetler, would you come to Sunday singing tomorrow evening, so that I can ask you to go on a buggy ride with me? I'd like nothing more than to court you."

Naomi's laughter was light on the afternoon air as she began to nod. "I'll probably have to pay a driver to get to singing, but it will be worth every penny if it means you'll be driving me home."

Just like that, it felt as if Edward's world shifted on its axis and turned towards the sun. Gone was the darkness of his father's disapproval, the loneliness of imagining a life with Naomi. He reached for her hand and gently brushed his lips over the top of it. "I'll be waiting for you at the barn door after singing."

Naomi laughed. "I'll be sure to find you there."

SECRETS AND SOUFFLES

*N*aomi's father was back on his feet.

After six months of taking things slow, doing his physical exercises, and walking with the walker as a precaution, he was finally almost back to his old self.

Just as it pleased Naomi to see her father back on his feet, it pleased Edward. Over the last six months, Edward had come not only to love Naomi dearly, but to respect and admire her father for the legacy he had built with the bakery.

Joseph was helping in the shop again when he felt up to it and often came to keep Edward company in the kitchen. It was clear Joseph's love for baking carried over to Naomi.

But tonight, wasn't about Joseph, Edward thought as he pulled up in front of the bakery with the buggy. Tonight, was about him and Naomi.

On the day of his brother's wedding, Edward had known deep inside his heart that the time would come for him and Naomi to start a future together. He hoped that tonight was that time. His heart was racing with anxiousness, although Edward already knew that Naomi would say yes.

But of course, there was always a chance she would say no.

He had planned the evening down to the very last detail. It was a full moon tonight, giving the landscape of Lancaster County a beautiful, magical, ethereal glow. He had packed a picnic basket with all her favorite things, as well as a bottle of sparkling grape juice. If everything went well, he would return home tonight an engaged man.

As he waited for Naomi, he thought about Bram and Lucy. They had just moved into the new home that Bram had built for them. Edward couldn't help but be baffled at how handy his father and his brother were. The house was a true work of art. It had three bedrooms, with extra room in the yard to expand later. The kitchen, dining room, and living room were all in one large open space, giving an airy feel.

Late afternoons, the large tree would cast a cool shadow over the porch, allowing you to watch the sunset in the shade. Edward frequently visited his brother at that time of day to catch up on their lives. He often missed not working with his brother anymore, not spending that time with him in the field. But Edward didn't miss the fields at all.

As things were, it was clear that Bram had proved himself to be a great farmer this year. They were only weeks away from harvesting, and it was bound to be another record year for the Fischer farm. Edward joined in his father's pride for Bram.

The bakery door opened, and Naomi stepped out. Although Edward had just seen her that morning, his tummy still fluttered with the anticipation of taking her on a buggy ride. To spend time with her without the interruption of customers or her father's presence.

To be just the two of them.

Edward climbed out and helped Naomi into the buggy. "You look very pretty tonight."

Naomi blushed slightly. "Just because I don't smell like cookie dough and flour in my hair."

Edward laughed as he took the reins. "Then you're even prettier!"

He drove the buggy towards the Amish settlement, knowing exactly where he wanted to ask for her hand. There was an outlook point on their property, near the tree line, that would give them a view of the entire town.

He had never brought her there before, saving it for this occasion.

When he brought the buggy to a stop, Naomi gasped with delight. "Edward, just look at the view. It's wunderbaar."

Edward agreed with a smile. "And to go with the view, all your favorite snacks."

He laid out a blanket for them to sit on before he unpacked the picnic. Naomi delighted him with tales of customers and baking disasters while they ate, Edward feeling too nervous to keep up his side of the conversation.

Eventually, Naomi picked it up. "Edward, is something wrong? You've barely spoken a word all night?"

Edward shook his head. "Nothing is wrong. Everything is just as it should be."

"Then why aren't you saying anything?" Naomi asked with a frown.

Edward chuckled. "Remember what I told you about courage at my brother's wedding?"

Naomi frowned for a moment before she nodded. "Jah, but you gathered it quickly enough."

Edward shrugged. "Tonight, took a little longer."

Edward stood up and pulled Naomi to her feet before he went down on one knee. He searched her eyes in the moonlight and felt that familiar rush of hope and courage spread through his veins.

"Naomi, there was a time when I didn't know how to be myself. A time when I was uncertain what I wanted from my future. But you changed all of that. Over the last six months, I've fallen in love with you, with baking and cooking, with the bakery, and with the relationship we have. I know what I want from my future, Naomi. I want to spend it with you. I want to bake with you, I want to have a familye with you, and I want us to grow the bakery and live full lives. Will you do me the honor of being my frau?"

Naomi's laughter was as light as the evening air. "Edward, of course I'll be your frau. But on one condition?"

Edward frowned, hoping it was something he could abide to. "And what is that?"

"You have to tell me the secret to these deviled eggs." Naomi reached for another one.

Edward laughed and shook his head. "A marriage should have no secrets, but a chef should at least have a secret or two in his arsenal of recipes."

Naomi pretended to pout. "In that case, I won't teach you how to bake a souffle."

"Then we'll be happily married with you baking souffles and me making deviled eggs," Edward said before he brushed a kiss over her lips.

On the land he didn't want to farm, he secured his future. A future with the woman he loved and a future pursuing his love for cooking.

THE NEXT GENERATION

"*D*aed, there is something Edward and I would like to talk to you about," Naomi said to Joseph on Monday afternoon.

They had just closed the bakery and Edward had agreed to stay later for the conversation they wanted to have with Joseph.

Joseph glanced from Naomi to Edward before he nodded in agreement. "Jah, we can talk. But not here. I'm tired of this small space. Let's go upstairs."

Naomi's heart stopped with fear. "Daed, are you sure you're ready to climb stairs? The doctor said…"

"The doctor said that if I'm up to it I can try. I've got both you and Edward here to help me if I struggle," Joseph said stubbornly, getting up from the chair in the office that had doubled as his bedroom for the last six months.

Naomi glanced at Edward who nodded at her encouragingly. "Of course, you're ready. But I'll walk behind you, just in case."

Naomi couldn't help but be fearful that her father would suffer a fall. But just like she was ready to entrust her future in Edward's hands, she trusted that he wouldn't let any harm come

90

to her father. She held back, giving her father and Edward room to pass her.

She watched as her father took the first step and couldn't help but hold her breath. Edward fell in behind her father, ready to act if needed.

For Naomi, the moment meant more than just giving her father a chance to try and get upstairs again. It was significant because Naomi knew that just like Edward stood behind her father, ready catch him if he fell, Edward would always be behind her.

For the rest of her life.

Her heart swelled with excitement to tell her father of their engagement.

She and Edward had agreed to tell their parents together; her father would be first.

When her father finally walked into the apartment upstairs, Naomi felt a wave of relief wash over her.

"There, and I'm still in one piece," Joseph said with a triumphant smile.

Naomi noticed the sweat beaded on his forehead, not knowing if it had been the exertion or anxiousness that had caused it. "I'll put on a pot of tea."

Edward followed her father to the living room. Naomi had gotten used to the empty space where her father's chair had always stood. Hopefully, soon, it would take its place in the living room again.

When Naomi returned with the tea, her father turned to her with a questioning look. "You had something you wanted to talk to me about?"

Naomi glanced at Edward before she turned to her father with a smile. "I'm sure you know that Edward and I have been courting for some time now?"

"Jah, I noticed something of the sort going on," Joseph said with a teasing smile.

"Edward asked for my hand, Daed, I accepted his offer of marriage," Naomi announced, feeling overjoyed to share the news with her father.

Joseph laughed; true joy expressed in his face. "That is just wunderbaar news. I hoped that something of the sort would come when I asked Edward to help you in the bakery."

"You did?" Naomi asked, surprised.

Her father nodded. "You've always been too busy to even consider courting, Naomi. Instead, Edward brought courtship to you. I'm happy for both of you. I trust that Gott will bless your marriage with love and the joy of kinner."

"Denke Daed. It means a lot to have your blessing." Naomi smiled warmly at her father.

"It's only a pleasure, mein dochder," Joseph said warmly before turning to Edward. "I know I don't have to tell you take gut care of her; I know you will."

Edward nodded. "With all my heart."

"Gut, now that you've shared your news, it's time for me to share mine." Joseph cleared his throat.

Naomi frowned, wondering what news her father had for them.

"You both know that I've joined the prayer group. I've found joy in reconnecting with the community after so many years of living on the outskirts. In addition to enjoying the company and the depth of faith we explore; I've enjoyed spending time with someone. Her name is Katrina Leipfuz. I too, have asked for her hand in marriage," Joseph announced with a naughty smile.

Naomi gasped with surprise. "You're engaged? You've been courting?"

"Jah, I am engaged. And nee, I wouldn't call it courting. At my age... I don't want to waste a minute when I already know what I want. I'm not asking for your blessing, but instead I'm asking you to take over the bakery. Completely."

"What?" Naomi asked, even more confused. She had always

known that she would one day inherit the bakery, but not while her father was still alive.

"I've spent my life between these walls, Naomi. I want to spend my golden years with Katrina. I want to help her in our kitchen garden, I want to drink tea on the porch, and I want to enjoy every moment of my health. Ever since I lost your mamm, I never thought I'd find love again. Now that I have, I want to cherish every second I have with Katrina. Besides, I know that I'm leaving the bakery in capable hands."

"That's kind of you to say, Joseph. I wish you and Katrina every happiness," Edward was the first to respond.

It took Naomi another moment to process everything before she knew wished her father the same. He had dedicated his whole life to Naomi and the bakery, and it was time for him to do something for himself.

"I'm happy for you Daed, I'm truly happy for you. I'd like to meet Katrina," Naomi smiled warmly at her father.

"We'll arrange Sunday lunch. With Edward of course. Once you're wed, you and Edward will live here, jah?"

Naomi shared a look with Edward before she nodded in agreement. "Of course. The baker of Hostetler Bakery always lives in the apartment above the bakery."

Naomi's heart was full as she smiled. She was surrounded by the two men she loved the most and knowing that her father had found love and happiness in his twilight years made her even happier.

ANOTHER CLOUD ON THE HORIZON

"*E*dward, this surely looks wunderbaar."

Edward smiled gratefully at his father's compliment. There had been a time when Edward hadn't thought he would ever be able to cook a meal for his father without his father's disapproval.

"Denke Daed. I thought a feast was in order to celebrate the harvest." Edward smiled across the table at his brother.

"Indeed," his mother agreed with a warm smile. "Here's to a record harvest for Fischer farm, and to my sons, of which I am very proud."

"Jah, to our sons and our dochder who will make us proud as well." Samuel lifted his apple juice in a toast.

"Denke Daed." Bram smiled at Lucy before he turned to the table. "And to Lucy, who is expecting our first born."

Congratulations sounded around the table. It was hard for Edward to remember that just a few months ago he wanted to be anywhere but having dinner with his family.

How much had changed, he realized, smiling at Naomi who sat beside him.

Edward drew in a deep breath before he made his and

Naomi's announcement. "Naomi and I also have something to share with you."

"You're engaged?" Daisy eagerly guessed.

Edward and Naomi's laughter gave them away. "Jah, we've become engaged," Edward agreed.

"And that's not all," Naomi interrupted him. "My daed has officially handed the bakery over to us. He is retiring to the community and giving Edward and I full control of the bakery."

"That is really gut news," Samuel said with a pleased smile. "I'm proud of you, Edward. I'm proud that you followed your dream, regardless of my foolishness. Joseph made the right decision; I know you and Naomi will take gut care of the bakery. We might have to discuss the bakery's name when you start having kinner, though."

Edward laughed, knowing what his father was hinting at. "I think Hostetler Fischer, is a little long for a bakery name."

Naomi thought for a moment before she smiled brightly at Edward. "But The Familye Bakery, isn't."

Everyone helped themselves to the feast at hand. Once everyone had a plate in front of them, Daisy cleared her throat. "Since it's an evening of announcements, I too have one to make."

The entire family turned to Daisy with curious looks. "What is it, Daisy?" Edwina finally asked.

Daisy drew in a deep breath. "I want you to keep an open mind," she said as warning. "You know the kinner I've been taking care of?"

"Jah?" her father asked, confused.

"They're off to start school soon. I hadn't thought past that just yet, but today something kind of made me think of it. I took the younger one to the doctor because he had a cold, and the doctor offered me a position as his assistant."

Edwina frowned and Samuel shook his head.

"The new Englisch doctor in town?" Bram asked curiously.

Daisy nodded. "He needs someone to make his appointments

and assist where necessary. He heard the twins were going to school and asked if I'd be interested. I told him I'd think about it, but I really think I should accept his offer."

"Daisy, you cannot work for an Englischer, that's where it all begins. They poison you with their worldly thoughts and before you know it, you prefer their world for ours."

"Daed, please. It's just a job. I'll have a chance to help people, more than just the twins I've been looking after."

"I think you'll do very well at being a doctor's assistant," Edward put in.

"Nee. No dochder of mine will work for an Englischer," Samuel said firmly.

Edwina let out a heavy sigh. "Samuel, we can at least give her a chance to see if she enjoys it?"

"Daed, I promise I won't let his thoughts affect my baptismal vows. This is something I really want to do. The wages are gut, I can contribute to the household..."

"Who will help your mother with the housekeeping chores?" Samuel all but growled.

"I'll still help. I will only be working there in the mornings, and I'll only start when the twins go to school. At least think about it, Daed?" Daisy pleaded.

Samuel shook his head. "I'm not discussing this tonight. Tonight, is for celebrating, not debating the downfall of my dochder's values and her place in this community." Samuel turned to his sons. "To Bram and Edward, you make your father's heart proud."

Edward smiled consolingly at Daisy. It wasn't too long ago that he was in her shoes. He understood his father's reservations but could only pray that his father would come to support her sooner than he had come to support him.

And just like Edward had to prove himself and have the courage to pursue his dreams, Daisy needed to do the same. He turned to Naomi and reached for her hand.

It didn't matter how many trials and tribulations he had to face with his father, it had been worth it now that he was engaged to the woman of his dreams.

The End

Thank you kindly for choosing to read my book. I sincerely hope you enjoyed it. All my Amish Romances are wholesome stories suitable for all to enjoy.

If you could be so kind to leave a review on Amazon, I would appreciate it.

Made in the USA
Thornton, CO
01/05/24 03:33:08